MILLENNIUM

MILLENNIUM

The
Seventh Day

By
Allen Bonck

 iUniverse®

MILLENNIUM
THE SEVENTH DAY

iUniverse books may be ordered through booksellers or by contacting:

iUniverse
1663 Liberty Drive
Bloomington, IN 47403
www.iuniverse.com
1-800-Authors (1-800-288-4677)

Because of the dynamic nature of the Internet, any web addresses or links contained in this book may have changed since publication and may no longer be valid. The views expressed in this work are solely those of the author and do not necessarily reflect the views of the publisher, and the publisher hereby disclaims any responsibility for them.

Any people depicted in stock imagery provided by Getty Images are models, and such images are being used for illustrative purposes only. Certain stock imagery © Getty Images.

ISBN: 978-1-6632-0178-2 (sc)
ISBN: 978-1-6632-0179-9 (hc)
ISBN: 978-1-6632-0177-5 (e)

Library of Congress Control Number: 2020911114

Print information available on the last page.

iUniverse rev. date: 06/25/2020

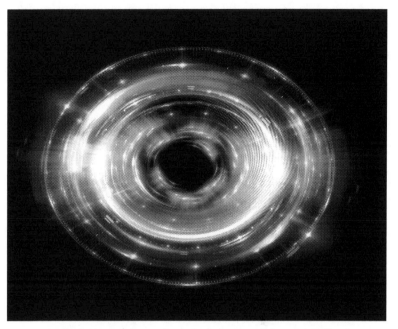

Artist conception of an Ophan angel [as described in chapter two]. Ophans are seen in the book of Ezekiel, and described as a wheel within a wheel.

Dedication

To my wife Linda, who has persistently encouraged me to write a prophetic fictional story using sound prophetic truths. She has been more than helpful

CONTENTS

CHAPTER ONE

The Day of the Lord

Just east of Jerusalem, a great portal opened in the sky! A turnpike of marvelous spiritual activity! The angel turned to the news crew and told them that the same things that are happening above them overhead, are also in five other portals around the world. Everyone below can only stare up to the heavens, awestruck.

Sean looking up asks, "What is it?" [1]

The angel answered, "That's Jacob's ladder. All these portals will be used by God's Host. When the armies reach the surface of the earth, they will become Joel's army and fight from point to point. In front of this army the land is green and beautiful but after God's army goes through the land, it will be black and burned. Jesus and his Bride will come first here to Petra which is Edom. Then on to Jerusalem." [2] [3] [4]

There were now great billows of fire unfolding around the opening in the sky. And lightning fired off continually around the host. This lightning was of all the colors of the rainbow, not at all natural. At the center of the host were a multitude of people on horseback wearing white robes, the Bride, with a single horseman leading them from the front. [5] [6]

There was the sound of the beating of a war drum a sound so deliberate and precise as to be felt inside your body. At first the source was not discernible, but as the procession came closer it was clear that the source was not a drum at all, but the hoofs of thousands of thousands of horses carrying the bride. [7] Every horse marching in perfect unison and rank as to be in time with the Lord's horse, by the time they could be seen clearly each hoof step sounded like thunder.

The angels and the host (armies of God) began to pour through. They came down swiftly and with purpose, creating streaks of light trails flowing through the sky. Their bearing was from east to west and they appeared to be tracking directly to Petra.

The rest of the heavenly hosts that followed were angels, Seraphim, Cherubim, and Ophanim. There weren't just a few thousand angels, there appeared to be millions! They were spreading out in every direction and obviously had assignments to accomplish. The angels traveled like lightning from point to point. The skies were lit up with their presence, all of this had the earth lit up brighter than noon day. There was a rumbling coming from deep in the earth.

When the heavenly army arrived at Petra, the horseman and host came down inside Petra from overhead! There was a period of silence for the Assyrian's troops outside the entrance to Petra. [8] They did not know whether to run or just hold their ground. Maybe this army was part of the Assyrian's forces? They didn't know. Suddenly, the blockade at the entrance of Petra, the two-story high concrete wall that was erected by the Assyrian to hold the Jews in Petra from escaping, suddenly it exploded from within, and then dissipated into nothing. Not even smoke was left. The heavenly army blew through the opening from within, like wind led by the Lord of the Host, the Elect One, Jesus!

The Assyrian's troops began to fall backward at the Lord's presence. Then everyone outside Petra which had the Assyrian's mark, the mark of the beast, were killed. God's angels were gathering the spirits of the slain as quickly as they could and leading them away. The heavenly army without hesitation turned north and proceeded toward Jerusalem, following the Lord of hosts

During the Lord's time in Petra before he blew open the blockade and destroyed the armies outside. The angels and his bride who are part of his entourage began to sing their praise to him.

"Holy, Holy, Holy, Behold the Lamb of God who removed the sins of the world by his blood. Behold his kingdom has come."

The people in Petra gathered to see Him. They looked up to Him in awe and began to join in to the praise. Everyone, Jews and gentiles in Petra worshipped him [9] [10]

Laura an American news reporter that had only recently become a believer and had come to Petra seeking refuge. She had come with her full crew, attempted to touch the muzzle of one of the huge and mighty horses of the bride. She flinched a little as its breath touched her skin. She touched its gleaming armor and hair. She returned her attention to the Lord who patted his horse's neck very gently. She saw Him leaned forward and whispered in its ear. Every muscle in the horse's body flexed and tightened. Then, suddenly the horse turned and made its way to Petra's exit, through the winding canyon.

A loud and bright explosion. The Bride and angels flowed out of Petra behind the Lord. The battle was on!

As the bright light of the Lord's presence disappeared, some of the angels remained with the people in Petra, to begin helping them prepare for their departure. The angel who had helped the American news crew to get to Petra several weeks earlier, approached the news crew.

"Do you have any questions?" asked the angel.

The news crew in unison answered, "Yes, millions."

The American news crew had come to Petra only about three weeks earlier They had been led there with the assistance of a team of God's angels. The news crew were from Washington D.C.

Eight years ago, the news crew had been assigned to investigate the disappearance of many people in America. They went to a small town in Oklahoma called Okusa, nearly everyone who lived in this town had disappeared without cause or trace. But the crew found information in one of the homes they had entered. They found Bible charts, books and papers, that indicated that the people had been removed by God as part of the resurrection of the dead, commonly called the rapture. The news crew did not believe any of the prophecy stuff because they were secular humanists, they basically mocked the author of the research. However, they decided to take the digitized research data to D.C. with them, and review it in detail. They began to see that the events found in the Oklahoma data was actually happening as indicated in the charts.

When they came to a point of the chart where it indicated that America would be destroyed next. While they did not believe the Bible prophecies, they left America after being encouraged in a dream by an angel. They still refused to believe in angels and God, however, when they got to Australia, they found that America had been destroyed while they were flying to Sydney. The destruction took place just as the Biblical prophecies had predicted.

The crew began to seek for a safe place to hide from the Assyrian's marking program. [11] The prophecy data which they were following, indicated that the only safe place was a natural stronghold located one hundred miles south east of Jerusalem, in modern Jordan, the land had been called Edom in ancient times and the fortress was an old abandoned rock city named Petra. A group of Jews and Christians had followed Jesus' admonition to flee to the wilderness when you see Jerusalem being surrounded by armies. [12] These refugees had been in Petra for over three years waiting for Jesus to deliver them. The news crew began to plan for their escape from Australia to Petra. They felt they needed to take supplies with them to Petra in hopes of buying their way into the fortress. But they could not through their own efforts get their plan to work. They ran into roadblocks. They finally prayed, they repented of their sins and asked for God's help., and he made a way for them.

Because the news crew were not believers until just weeks before arriving in Petra, God's angels began to educate them about the things of God right after arriving. The crew had no idea about God or who God is. The large contingent of Jews and Christians who were in Petra from the beginning of the siege, had years to be trained in what to expect when Jesus returns to set up a kingdom. The angels taught the crew about the creation of the world and how it is held together.

They learned that the world is basically empty, there is nothing here, 99.99% empty. The Atoms of the world are held together by energy and nothing else. The energy was provided by the Elect One, Jesus, at the time of creation. He, Jesus is still maintaining that energy and holding the world together. The bible teaches that in him all things consist. The Biblical word "consist" means: "to be held or bound [13] together". His power is in his words. He is seen in Revelations chapter nineteen on his horse, and he has a sword coming from his mouth. When he speaks, energy can be removed from the atoms, which he targets and they simply disappear, nothing left not even visible dust. This is why the Assyrian soldiers just outside Petra disappeared as Jesus went by, and their spirits gathered to sheol, the place of the dead.

Because the news crew had worked for years as a team before coming to Petra, they were allowed to camp together within Petra. Everyone in Petra had an open-air area to live in, and some caves in the city walls to shelter in when they had the need. Petra was an open-air city with stone buildings and streets, they had by and large been reduced to rubble by the twenty first century. However, the walls of Petra were carved with building facades and chambers within the rock walls. The chambers were used by the ancients primarily as tombs for their dead. The current Jews in Petra had enlarged the chambers to accommodate their supplies and equipment.

Because the news crew had come very late in the siege, they were given their chamber in a place slightly removed from the other people. They placed their equipment in their own chamber. They came to Petra with a multitude of cameras, recorders, video cameras, lap top computers and data storage equipment. Also, all the tripods, lenses, microphones and batteries, they even had manual and solar battery chargers if they had the need.

The news crew was pretty ordinary. It consisted of six members. The director is Sean Wright, he is now 36 years old, there is no doubt that he is in charge of the crew although he seems perpetually stressed. Sean is 5'10" with intense blue eyes short blond hair.

Laura Thornton, 31 years old is the reporter/journalist, she's the attractive lady that gives the report. She's a slim 5'-8" with mid length blond hair and fair complexion, she's definitely camera ready.

Evelyn Odel, the communications expert. Evelyn looks like the girl next door, 5'-6" with short brown hair and dark brown eyes. She has a Mediterranean complexion.

Isaac Warren, video camera operator. He's a British born, 31-year-old Englishman, black hair combed straight back, with hazel eyes. He's tall and lanky, but still athletic. Isaac was the first one in the crew to be contacted by one of God's angels.

Sally Hamilton, the still camera photographer. She could be Laura's younger sister, except she's a little shorter and after the past eight years her hair is darker. Coloring her hair seemed so meaning less to her while the world and its nations were systematically being destroyed.

The sixth and last member is Gus G. Hubbard the crew's investigator. He's now 50, a no non-sense man with dark brown eyes and brown hair and a big man, 6'-2", 200 lbs. and with a perpetual five o'clock shadow. As a young man Gus was an army ranger, an occupation which is only for the young. He had just divorced before the war, and was not happy about it. Gus is honest to a fault. He had struggled more than the other crew members with the Bible prophecies and with God in general.

The most amazing thing about the news crew was how well they worked together. There were many times they disagreed on what to do or how to respond, but they seemed to have mutual respect for each other. The immensity of the events they were witnessing caused them to get closer and to trust each other, they bonded and focused on their goals. The very fact that they were not killed during the war attests to this unity. They did not lose any one of the members, no small feat.

The angel that was talking to the crew smiled when he heard the crew's response, "Yes millions". The angel turned and beckoned for a young man to approach them. The young man came over. He had a white robe on.

"He is from the bride of Christ." The angel said.

Gus reached out to shake the young man's hand.

Isaac shook his hand as well. "It's a pleasure to meet you, Mr. ... I'm sorry. I didn't get your name"

The man replied, "Oh, it was Thomas Taylor."

The crew suddenly fell silent.

"Did you say Thomas Taylor?" Sally said looking at Thomas intently.

He nodded.

"That's the same name as the Oklahoma prophesy man." Isaac said. "The man who wrote the prophecy studies which served as the guide for us thru the tribulation period and judgment of the nations."

"It can't be him. We know for a fact that he'd be pushing seventy years old." Laura said perplexed.

"I know it's a silly question but, might you be his son?" Evelyn asked.

Thomas replied, "No, I never had a son."

The crew's mouths were all agape. Isaac turned with laughter. "This is our Tom! He changed just like the scripture said he would!" Isaac exclaimed. "He truly is resurrected,"

Laura gave Thomas a hug. She cupped his face in her hands to admire it.

"Yes, Thomas is in his prime again, only better. He will never age. Death is swallowed up in victory!" said the angel. [14]

Thomas said, "I'm grateful that you were able to use my collection of data. It had taken me decades to put it together."

"We could not have succeeded if it hadn't been for you, Tom." Sean added.

Thomas responded "You're too kind but I had only assembled the data with the Holy Spirit's help, the truth all came from God's word."

The angel walked away, the crew and Tom turned to see where he was heading.

He turned to them, "It's time to go home, to Jerusalem. We all have work to do." Said the angel.

CHAPTER TWO

The Witness

As they begin to traverse through Petra to their encampment on the far edge. An angel appeared to them in their path. This angel is not one of the angels which had been their guides in the past. This angel was all business, his eyes were very intense, he is in battle mode.

He turns to Gus, and says "The Lord has need of you in Jerusalem"

Gus responds, "Yes I understand that we are getting ready to go there."

The angel replies, "You are to come with me, you only, not your friends."

Almost instantly Gus and the angel disappear. They don't go far, just to the other end of Petra. They came to a group of men and some angels. Gus quickly estimates that there are about a dozen men and three angels, the men and Gus are gathered into a circle facing outward and told to lock arms. Suddenly they were all surrounded by a shield of light. They were being held very tightly. They began to rise into the sky very gently until they were several hundred feet above Petra, they stopped and paused for a moment, then like a flash of lightning they took off. Before Gus could figure out what had happened, they were at the Temple mount in Jerusalem 100 miles north of Petra and gently touching down.

Gus estimates to himself that the elapsed time for the travel was less than one second. He felt a release, and the light moved away. Gus turned to see where it went. What he saw astounded him. It is a large orb of light with eyes all around the inside. There are wheels of fire and light inside the orb. It moved and pulsed like it is alive. Gus was so impressed that he could not quit smiling, suddenly he realized that the eyes of the creature were looking at him. At first, he felt embarrassed then he realized that the creature was smiling back! Somehow, he could see it in his eyes, Gus nodded and saluted the creature. [15]

Gus looked around to see what the other passengers were doing. Some were in shock. And others were talking to each other, they did not seem to understand what had happened.

"Mr. Hubbard," he heard the Angel say, "please come with me, we're on a schedule"

Gus was led to a tent on the south end of the temple mount. He was shown a seat and asked to sit. The other men who came with him from Petra were also filing in. "Mr. Hubbard," The angel says, "I am assigned to be your interpreter, the other men here all know Hebrew and can take instruction directly from the angel in charge, I will help you understand what is happening."

Gus responds to the angel, "Sir, can you give me the target objectives?"

The angel stops and looks at Gus sand says, "You're a seal?"

"No, I was a ranger" say's Gus.

The angel has a relieved look on his face, "This is going to make my job much easier".

The angel begins to explain things to Gus. "In the Biblical book of Micah, in chapter five, [16] the Lord promised to deliver the city of Jerusalem from the Assyrian antichrist. He has done that today, Bet Sharrukin is dead. Jesus also promised the Jews that they could participate in the destruction of the land of Assyria. That part of his promise is about to happen. The

Lord had said that he would raise up 15 men to go with him to Assyria to judge that land."

Gus Questions, "Are we going to engage the Assyrians ourselves, if so, these men that came with me will need some training."

The angel replies, "No, you will not be asked to engage the enemy. The Lord always has witnesses to his acts, he never does anything without having others there to witness his actions. This is normally done by his angels. [17] There are angels which are trained to record the events for God. This is to confirm the truth when it is required during the great judgment." The Holy scriptures indicate that judgment will be made on every word spoken. [18]

The angel continues, "The Lord has chosen twelve Jewish men from Petra, one man from each of the twelve tribes. He has also chosen three non-Jewish men to join with them to witness the faithfulness of God to his people and to his word. Mr. Hubbard, you have been honored by God to be one of his witnesses, this is a great honor."

Gus is not sure what to say, he's completely new to God things and can't understand why God would choose him for anything at all. He does not yet understand that God see's things differently than men do. God looks to the heart, the deeper things of man.

The lead angel turns to Gus's angel and points to the door and say's something. The angel with Gus indicates that he should follow him. They go next door to another enclosure where Gus is shown the mikveh. These are ritual baths for purifying the body, the angel explains that it is necessary before they leave, because there is always a chance that they may be required to speak to the Lord himself. Gus will also be given a new set of clothes to wear, for the same reason. You don't just show up to see God, the one that created all heaven and earth without some preparation.

When Gus see's the clothes that he is to wear his countenance drops. This is not what an Army ranger wears when going into a battle theater.

Gus thinks, *"I know I won't be required to participate, but I have not worn anything like this since I was a choir boy."*

The angel steps aside and consults with the lead angel for a few minutes, and returns.

"Mr. Hubbard, The Lord say's that you are not one of the Jews, and thus you and the other two Gentiles will be allowed to choose your own garments from the racks provided, subject to our approval."

"When did you talk to the Lord?" Gus asked. "He heard your thoughts from a moment ago, and did not want you to be unhappy about your assignment. He told us in the Spirit to help you."

Gus is shocked, he had never considered how intimate God can be with his people. He thinks to himself, *"I'm not in D.C. any more, the world has changed, I need to be careful, I can't think the way I used to".*

Gus chooses an earth tone shirt with long sleeves and has no collar; the shirt extends below his waist. He also has breeches made of a slightly tougher material, covering the thighs down to his feet. When the angel sees him, he studies him closely then nods his approval. He then tosses Gus a pair of tall stout boots. This time Gus nods his approval back.

The men are led back into the briefing tent and the lead angel continues the instructions. Through his interpreter Gus is told that this campaign is a judgment upon the enemies of God. That the people with the mark of the beast will be destroyed without recourse. The believers had been removed during the resurrection and only the unbelievers and the backslidden remain in the theater. There may be some people who were not believers but also did not submit to the marking system of Bet Sharrukin, the Assyrian antichrist. They may be removed from the destruction, but only at the discretion of Jesus himself. The witnesses should make mental notes of all they see, and during breaks in the action they can write notes. They can also dictate to a group of recording angels during the heat of the battle.

Suddenly, word came that the perimeter of the battle theater has been established and they are ready for the witnesses. The angel led the men to a waiting ophan, the wheel of fire that brought them to Jerusalem. They begin to assemble and lock arms to load into the wheel, Gus is studying everything he can about the creature. He feels warm but not hot or burning like you would expect being so close to the flames. He thinks, *"How do they do this?"* But before he can surmise an answer, they are off and only a second later, following the now familiar pattern and landing on a floating platform.

As soon as they are released by the chariot of fire, they are informed that they are in southern Babylon, what is Biblically called the land of Nimrod at the entrance to Babylon. In modern terms this is southern Iraq. The perimeter that the angels have established is completely around the entire nation of Iraq, portions of northern Iran and southern Turkey.

The platform they are standing on has rails across the front and seats just behind. The witnesses are given seats and told to watch out the front. This command platform is not visible to anyone in the natural world. The platform is now in the spirit world, it can enter the natural world if needed, but not during normal operations. The platform moves very quickly in all directions. Gus estimates that the current altitude is about eight thousand feet above the deck. [19]

The Lord is below the platform and directly in front, he is still in his blood-stained war garments which he was wearing in Petra a few hours earlier. His bride is still with him, fanning out behind him in echelon, still on their horses. They are all waiting to move.

Then Jesus waved his arms outward and then to each side. Gus's angel tells him that this is the signal for a group of angels to be sent out. These angels are being sent to locate and extract anyone that the Lord does not want to be killed. The angels are being led to the hiding spots of these people by the Holy Spirit. The Holy Spirit knows where every single person is, within the theater. He also knows where they are underground, he will direct the angels to find and extract them. When They are safely in God's control a bright light is seen at the recovery location. While these people are not in danger from the Lord, if the people who have the mark of the beast get to these people before the angels, they will kill them out of hatred.

The angels are moving into the theater from all sides at the same time, to reduce the time for the enemy to communicate their operation.

Only moments after the operation commences lights are flashing down below. When each one is seen the angels give a shout, "another soul saved from hell" and they cheer. It is still sobering to realize that so few are being found. Very few have been able to survive the full 3 1/2 years of total Antichrist control.

The platform follows along behind the angels as they clear the people. Gus sees some of the people being brought past the platform, sometimes entire families holding each other. They don't look happy, they look terrified.

Gus asks the angel, "Why are they so unhappy?" The angel responds, "They're not sure whether they are being taken to be executed or not. They won't know for sure until they are shown love, even then it will take time for it to sink in."

"What will happen to them now?" Gus ask's, "They will be taken to Jerusalem and processed. They will be cared for and offered a place within God's kingdom. They will be required to go under Jesus' royal scepter, which means they will submit to his rule and authority. [20] They of course don't have to do it, but we think they will."

After about two hours of extractions, the angels meet at the center of the theater.

Gus's angel says, "This phase is the most tedious of the whole operation because so much care is given to the people being extracted, the second phase is faster, but much more violent. We will reset our location back to the perimeter and start the attack from there, The Lord does not want anyone over the theater."

Gus asks, "Will this be a total destruction?"

The angel replies, "No, only those things which are profane will be dissolved. The land, trees, rivers and such will be spared damage when possible. Phase two removes all the demons and spirits from the theater. This will blind the enemy to a large extent, because only the spirits and fallen angels can see the actual battle. It will start with a call to the fallen angels to surrender and go to a specific coordinate for incarceration. There will be a lot of weeping and tears among them, but the Lord only allows them five minutes to respond. They will be bound and taken away for judgment." [21]

Suddenly all that the angel had been describing was taking place right in front of them. The fallen angels rising from the earth and demons flying like birds in great flocks, all moving

15

towards a collection of enclosures floating high in the air over head.

Gus thinks to himself, *"How can all those spirits and angels go into those few enclosures?"* Then he remembered that they are spirits and the world is empty space.

The angel turns to Gus, and nods. He say's "You're right". He continues, "there are a multitude of underground facilities and bases throughout the theater. Most of them are full of Rephaim. The Rephaim are more advanced technologically than the Enoshe and must be approached with more care."

The Angel is interrupted by a wave of energy proceeding from the Lord and his bride out through the land. It had the appearance of a wall of dirt and dust. It was rumbling from deep in the earth, as the dust began to settle behind the wave large sections of the land appeared to be plowed up from deep within the earth. The areas that were plowed showed signs of concrete structures and equipment within the rubble. Almost immediately the remnants of these underground facilities simply disappeared, concrete, equipment, everything gone.

Gus asked, "Why did it disappear, couldn't something be salvaged?"

The angel replies, "Nothing that has been made or used by the Rephaim or Enoshe will exist on the earth when the purge is finished, it is all unclean and must be dissolved.

As the underground destruction continues to proceed across the land, Gus turns to the angel and states, "I'm sorry Sir, but I don't know who you are talking about when you say, Rephaim or Enoshe. Can you please explain?"

"Yes of course, I should have known that most people don't understand the terms, you and your news crew are completely new to these things."

The angel continues, "First the term "Enoshe" is the Hebrew name given to fallen man during the early days of your race. Enoshe are the children of Adam and Eve. You Gus are an Enoshe. You have been redeemed by the blood sacrifice of Jesus at the cross, you are now able to enter into the kingdom because you are clean, but all of your works which were done before have no place in the kingdom. God's new kingdom on earth is completely new and fresh."

"The second term "Rephaim" is the name of a group or race of giants, which were first created by intercourse between some fallen angels and the [22] daughters of Adam. Their children became the "lawless ones" they began to destroy the Enoshe and sinned against creation itself. They ruled the world for about 500 years until they were destroyed by God at the flood. The Giants or Nephilim all died at the flood, but their Spirits, continued to live as disembodied spirits after the flood. Most, about 90% of the Spirits were [23] [24] arrested by God and incarcerated in a pit with their fathers the angels. The remaining 10% of the spirits are left free to vex mankind. They will be collected and incarcerated at the end of the age. Which of course is right now, it is happening right in front of you."

"Why have I never heard of them" asked Gus.

The angel replies, "When the Israelites were coming out of Egypt, it was called the exodus. The Israelites found the land of Canaan full of Rephaim tribes and cities. It was these giants that scared the Jew's from entering into the land.

After an additional forty years, the Israelites were allowed to leave the wilderness, the Negev desert, and move towards the land given to them by God. We were sent before them to clear the way., mainly spiritually, but we also attacked the Rephaim and drove them out from before God's people. The Rephaim had already been living underground in caves because they feared us. They had become bolder because the Jew's had been living in Egypt for 450 years. Rephaim were Biblically called the "Zuzims", giant wild beasts, "Zamummins" those who imagine evil thoughts, "Emins" giant terrors, "Anakim" long necked giants, and "Horims" cave dwellers.

We drove nearly all the Rephaim out of Israel and they fled to remote locations all over the earth. Their fathers are the fallen angels of Satan or Lucifer. They took many gentile tribes with them to these remote areas as workers and slaves. These people saw the giants as god's and willingly served them.

The Rephaim had close relations with their angel fathers and were given access to high levels of technology. They were flying aircrafts all over the world before the time of Christ. They also knew that if they attacked or harassed God's people, the Jews and later the Christians. That God would send us, his angels to punish them. They never intentionally made contact with God's people. They would occasionally take DNA from people for research.

Gus interrupts, "Wait a minute, are you saying that the Alien's and their space craft, you know, the UFO's are Rephiam? "Yes, of course"

Gus again asks, "So they're not from outer space at all?"

"Correct, they are creatures from a complex race of half angel and half man hybrids that have existed with mankind from Adam's days. They know they will be judged at the end of this age and not allowed to enter Christ's kingdom."

Today is their judgment, they will cease to exist as a race.

Gus quietly responds, "I did not understand the gravity of the moment", Thank you for the explanation"

The angel nods and says, "You will have a lot of time to learn the details."

As the energy wave moves toward the center of the theater, large numbers of surface to air weapons can be seen coming towards the energy wave, it's obvious that they intend to strike beyond the wave. As these weapons pass over the ground wave they are dissolved by a secondary source from the Lord. Some of the weapons simply go out of control, begin to spin and impact the ground inside the perimeter.

When the attack began to dwindle, like the end of a fireworks display. The Lord and his Host begins to move forward from the south to the north. It seems to Gus that the progress is very slow, but he realizes that because of the altitude of his observation platform and the fact that the platform is actually moving as well, the progress is faster than 100 miles per hour. As they move forward over the land, everything that was man made disappeared like smoke, no people, no building, no cars, no roads or bridges, nothing left.

Within hours the Lord arrives at Nineveh in northern Iraq, Assyria. The city and its modern partner, Mosul, are completely razed. The observation deck is lowered to a couple of hundred feet above the ground so that the witnesses can see, that nothing is left, only the rivers. The Jewish witnesses begin to cheer and shout alleluia to the Lord our God and to his kingdom. [25]

As Gus watched, he saw the Lord stop all talking and activities. He is only about 30 feet in front of the observation platform. He turns to the land of Assyria and raises his arms and he begins to speak a blessing over the land.

When he is done, Gus asks, "He just destroyed the land completely and now he blesses it? What just happened?"

The angel replies, "No, he didn't destroy the land, he purged the land. He destroyed all that was in the land that had defiled it. The land is now free to recover from man's sin and abuse.

The seventh day, the earths sabbath has now begun, the rocks are free to cry out and praise him.

The Lord dismounts his horse and moves towards the Witnesses. As he is coming Gus's angel turns to Gus and ask's, "Mr. Hubbard, would you be willing to continue as a witness for the Lord, as he continues his campaigns against the world's nations? The duration is not fixed, but it will take approximately four days to finish. If not, you can return to Jerusalem or join with your news friends and walk up to Jerusalem."

Gus could not be happier, while he likes his friends, being on the front lines of God's army is amazing. He says "I would like to stay here and do whatever the Lord needs." Gus looks down sheepishly and says, "Sir, can you please call me Gus instead of Mr. Hubbard?"

Before the angel could answer, the Lord himself entered the area. Everyone had bowed to their knees'; he raised them and began addressing the witnesses in Hebrew. Gus looked to his angel for an interpretation, but he just indicated that Gus should look at the Lord. As Gus turned to look at the Lord, he heard the Lord say, "Gus, I can speak English when needed, thank you for your assistance, and your desire to continue your assignment. Your name is no longer Gus G. Hubbard, you are now, Audee-el. Welcome to the Kingdom." [26]

The Lord quickly turns and walks toward the other end of the platform.

Gus is left speechless, he can only stare straight forward, then after some moments of silence he finally asks the angel, "What does it mean? My new name, what does it mean?"

The angel replies, "Audee means a witness, and El means God's. You are God's witness." It is pronounced "audee-el".

The angel continued, "welcome to the team Audee-El, let's go."

CHAPTER THREE

The Morning Stars

Back in Petra the news crew are waiting for the Jewish tribes to finish getting assembled, to leave Petra. The crew had been informed that they would be following the Jewish tribes.

The tribes are being arranged based on the arrangement from the book of Revelations, as they were sealed on mount Sion in Jerusalem, Juda, Reuben, Gad, Asher, Nepthalim, Manasses, Simeon, Levi, Issachar, Zabulon, Joseph, and Benjamin. Each tribe is flying their own banner. [27]

The crew was also told that they were to bring nothing out of Petra with them, not even a comb. Everything they will need, will be provided to them as they exit Petra.

The idea that they are to leave all they have behind is not easy to swallow. They only have the very basic possessions for life anyway, and now they are told to leave everything behind? It only gets tougher when they realize that this includes their equipment. Their equipment which represents who they are, they're a news team, how can they do their job without their tools?

Sean, in an attempt to be pragmatic, reminds the others that they should be thankful that they are among the survivors of the battle, and should remain flexible. This position is met with varying degrees of skepticism.

Finally, Laura Thornton the reporter says, "He's right we need to remember where we were and what's been done for us. We may be able to return and get our equipment at some later time."

"Well that settles it", Isaac says, "if Laura can walk away from her beauty stuff so can I."

This comment draws a smile from Sally, and everyone concurs that they will cooperate.

One of the angels assigned to them comes over and sets down with them. They can tell that he has something he wants to tell them.

"I heard your conversation, and want you to understand that the new world, the new kingdom is very much different than the one that is being destroyed outside Petra. You need to understand that the transition from the old to the new will be difficult at times. Please know that all decisions being made concerning you and your future, are being made with you in mind. The Lord knows and loves everyone who is in his earthly kingdom. He has a lot to do in establishing the new world after the war. The day of the Lord, is over, the reconstruction of the world is of the utmost importance to all of us. Your talents and efforts will be needed for the tasks at hand, no one is excluded."

A second angels speaks up, "Within the supplies that you will get when you exit Petra, is a pad and pencil, meant for you to write your thoughts and for keeping a journal for yourself. This may help you with your reporting tendencies"

Laura thinks to herself, *"My tendencies? My tendencies, what does that mean? Good grief"*.

Sally blurts out, "Where is Gus? Where have you taken him? I want to know!"

The other members of the crew jerk to attention and turn to Sally, evidently, they were not very concerned about Gus. He can take care of himself. But it seems that Sally has come to lean on Gus for support. She is not the least bit happy about his absence.

The second angel looks to the first angel, he is given a nod. He says, "I cannot actually tell where he is at this moment, because I don't know. However, a few moments ago he was leaving Assyria and proceeding to Europe, I'm not at liberty to tell you where. Gus has joined an operation that will take him all over the world. At this time, he expects to be back with you all before you reach Jerusalem."

Sally is mollified, she feels a little embarrassed. The rest of the crew acknowledges the information, Isaac says, "cool".

As the crew resumes their sitting and waiting positions, they notice more spiritual activity crossing Petra overhead. Most of the activity seems to be coming down outside Petra, just to the south, it's been happening for hours.

Evelyn concerned, says, "I hope that it's safe to leave the stronghold. Maybe that's why we're not going out, it might not be secure out there yet."

Sean replies, "No I don't think so, I think that moving all these tribes in one direction, all these people, is like trying to herd cats., it just takes time. These people have been cooped up in this place for 3 ½ years, they are really excited. It's only been hours since the Lord was right here in Petra."

Finally, they began to move forward towards the exit, the long thin canyon which leads to the outside, it's called the "siq" by the Arabs. The siq is very narrow and can only accommodate 4 or 5 people across. This is in part responsible for the slow going. It is like having 4 football stadiums full of people all trying to exit thru one exit. But there is another reason, when the people move through the siq, they are given a backpack with things in it for the journey.

Each pack has their name and number plainly written on it. The number is the camping location in the facilities outside

23

Petra. Each person is given a small map of the camp to assist them in finding their location.

Food and water stations are mixed into each of the areas, no one has to travel very far to get to them. They are designated for the camps according to they're numbers. The baths and latrines are the same way.

The long-term residents of Petra are in tears as they explore the camp. Everything is clean and sanitary; the beds are made with clean linen and are off the ground. Each sleeping compartment is also raised off the desert floor. These facilities are more like hotel rooms than a desert bivouac. Each group of compartments have chairs and a table outside the units.

The crew is amazed as they walk to their tents and personal area.

Sally says; "How did they build this camp in just hours?"

Sean adds; "Now we know what's been going on out here. Most of the facilities look like they are modular and assembled on site. I've never seen these kinds of building materials before."

Within each of the dwelling units is a set of instructions to help the people understand how the next day will go. It is basically an itinerary complete with wake-up time and breakfast. What to carry with them and what items to leave behind in the morning. Every unit has clothes for each person to put on after they take their baths in the morning, any complaints will be addressed at the end of the first day hike. Everyone's old clothes are to be left behind in the unit.

The instructions include a list of shofar calls to lead assembly for everyone. The shofar is the ancient rams horn trumpet used in the past.

After the crew had eaten dinner, bathed and were sitting outside their tent, Isaac began laughing, everyone wondered what his problem was.

Sean asked, "Alright, what's so funny?"

Isaac turns to the crew, "I'm wondering how Gus is going to do with the new clothes. I just can't imagine Gus in these clothes."

The whole group gets a good laugh.

Sally says, "For what it's worth, I've been told that these clothes can be changed once the war is over and the circumstances settle down."

As the crew is talking, the angels, two of them, came walking up to the camp.

Evelyn asks, "Where have you been? We had not seen you since we entered the siq."

The angels acknowledged Evelyn and said "Busy, very busy, how do you like your accommodations?"

The crew chimes in together, "They're great, we feel almost human again."

Evelyn looks at the angels and asks, "Is it possible for us to know your names? We've been resisting giving you names so we can keep things straight when we're talking about you. But we would really like to know your names"

The angel which originally contacted Isaac before the war stepped forward, "In the past we angels were to never reveal ourselves to people, we supported, protected and ministered to your needs, as we were directed by the Holy Spirit. We are ministering spirits to the heirs of salvation, the unseen hand behind the scenes. We were never to divert any credit to ourselves. The people, the saints of God had to live by faith, not by sight. Faith is the evidence of things not seen. If we were constantly showing ourselves it could compromise their faith, and this must never happen. We could not show ourselves without a direct order from the Lord, he knows what is best, he would also limit our conversations and actions according to his wisdom."

A second angel speaks, "Since the Lord has revealed himself to the entire world, the spiritual dynamics around faith and our ministry to men has changed, we are much more open and freer to directly communicate with you and others. The Lord is trusting us to conduct ourselves with wisdom and discretion as we work."

The first angel continues, "After thousands of years of non-contact many angels are not comfortable giving, they're names, to the Enoshe, man. It is now completely up to each angel as to whether or not they will release their names."

The second angel speaks again, "You need to understand that angels are assigned tasks and then reassigned to a new task without warning. We may be reassigned tomorrow and someone else taking our places. We will let you all know tomorrow if anyone of us will tell you our names."

The first angel tells the news crew, "Come with me. I think you will like this."

They all begin to stroll down through the camp. As they stroll, the crew notices that the other angel has departed. They also can hear some sounds coming from further into the camp. Some young teen age Jewish boys go running past them weaving through the people. Sean sees another group of young people running by, he reaches and grabs one of the runners, Sean asks, "What's going on? Why are you running?" The young man pulls away and turns to Sean and shouts, "The morning stars! The morning stars are singing! At the intersection."

Sean turns to the angel, and as they continue walking the angel explains, "The morning stars, the angels, originally sang praises to God at the time of creation. They have now been praising God for thousands of years in heaven. It is who we are, our love for God cannot be contained in mere words spoken, we must sing his praises. Sometimes it is scheduled, but most times it is spontaneous. Tonight, is not spontaneous, we have been waiting to see this day for thousands of years, the day that we can praise God openly before everyone on earth. The angels looked forward to the day that God's will, will be done in earth as it is in heaven, we knew it meant that we could praise God openly on earth, and we intend to do it." [28]

The angel begins to walk away, then turns back to the crew and says, "We will sing most of the songs in Hebrew, but some will be in our language, the tongues of angels." He turns and disappears.

The crew continues to the center of the camp, except now they have quickened their step, they have some anticipation. When they reach the center, to say there is some excitement is an understatement. The people are talking, pointing and looking around.

Then suddenly at the precise moment that the sun goes down and the next day begins, the first day of the new world, there was a trembling coming from the earth, a deep rumbling from below, but not just below, it was also coming from the rocks on the outer walls of Petra. All the talking stopped and the people listened. The shaking was not like an earthquake because there was rhythm to the vibrations, it was not natural. The stones began to crack and fracture in sequences like notes in a song, the rocks are crying out. The earth cannot contain its liberation from man's sin, it must praise God.

A circle at the center of the intersection had been cordoned off from the people, it is 200 feet in diameter.

As the Earth begins to attenuate its song, a circle of Ophanim appears at the center of the intersection they are 20 feet in diameter and each touching the other. They are in a circle

20 feet inside the cordoned off area. They are the chariots of fire, the wheels within a wheel of Ezekiel chapter one, they are providing the foundation of a platform for the Angelic orchestra to sit on top of them. They are all in their transfigured appearance, the angelic equivalent to a Marines dress whites.

The angelic orchestra is full of instruments of all kinds, many that have never been seen by men before, some of the instruments look somewhat like instruments made by man. But mostly they are new, the only thing really the same, is that some of them use strings and others are horns and some, are like drums.

A very large angel rises up above the orchestra, and begins to address the camp, in a loud, yet precise voice.

"Fifty years from now on the jubilee, someone will ask you, (now he shouts) were you there on that night, the first night of the new world! When the Ben Elohim shouted praise unto our God, and the people cried Amen, Amen, Amen!

Were you there when the morning stars sang praises to the King of Kings and the Lord of Lords? And you will say, yes, yes, we were there!"

As he finished his statement, he dropped his arms and the orchestra, all in unison struck a single note. Then above the orchestra was a tier of angel singers, they matched the same note perfectly, then above those angels was another tier of angels suddenly appearing above them. The orchestra and new tier struck a different note. Then a third tier and a third note. This process repeated itself seven times, each tier on top of the last, cantilevering over the last until the angels made a canopy over the camp. There were thousands and thousands of them.

When the tiers reached the top, the song started again at the bottom each note rising, but now with words. The tribes erupted with cheers because they had been learning this song from the angels for the past three years.

PRAISE GOD FROM WHOM ALL BLESSINGS FLOW...
PRAISE HIM ALL CREATURES, HERE BELOW...
PRAISE HIM ABOVE, YE HEAVENLY HOST...
PRAISE FATHER, SON, AND HOLY GHOST...
AMEN.... AMEN... AMEN.

They continued singing, praising and worshipping God, song after song, in perfect pitch tempo and clarity. Some songs were in Hebrew and others were done in unknown languages, that only the angels understood. The angels themselves would often change colors with the songs, sometimes they would bow their heads and go dim in humility, and then light up again when they sang of God.

Every song spoke to the greatness of God, to his faithfulness and mercy. At times the Holy Spirit would flow out from the angels and cover the camp, the glory of God like a luminescent cloud would flow through the people, submerging and baptizing them. God's presence was overwhelming. [29]

Then, after about two hours, the finale, the opening song, the doxology, was repeated in reverse order, each tier would sing its word and disappear, from top to the bottom, ending with each "AMEN" fading away.

When the orchestra and Ophanim disappeared, there remained not a sound, not a word. The people quietly turned and made their way home. The peace of God covered the camp like a blanket.

CHAPTER FOUR

The Journey Begins

"Sean... Sean, wake up," Isaac calls through the compartment door. "The Shofar has sounded and the people are leaving, you're late, you're late!"

Sean launches out of the bed, grabs his clothes and starts dressing, hair is still sticking straight out and only one shoe latched, he flies out the door and looks to see where everyone has gone.

The crew is sitting at the table outside having breakfast, they look up to see Sean and they crackup laughing.

Sean asks, "Where is Isaac! I'll get him!" He turns to see Isaac standing to his right against the wall, Isaac is trying to catch his breath, from laughing so hard.

Isaac says, "Wait a minute, I told you that the Shofar has sounded, and that the people are leaving, and that you are late. That's all true. I may have exaggerated the urgency of the moment a little. But if it weren't for me you would still be sleeping."

The rest of the crew said, "Yes, yes he's right, you should thank him."

Sean lets out a sigh, smiles at the crew, and gives Isaac a fist bump. Then he turns back to his compartment and says, "I'm going in. to start over".

After a short-time Sean comes out, properly dressed and cleaned up, he sits down with the rest of them and begins his breakfast, then he asks?" So, what time is it anyway?"

The crew all look at each other and smile, then Isaac says, "We have no idea".

Sean replies, "Okay now what's going on?"

Isaac says, "We're not pulling your leg, The Angels informed us just a few moments ago that our old, time keeping system is now defunct. Evidently it had its origins from the old Egyptian religion, way back when. And that since sundown last night the earth will be using the system ordained by God before the flood, Noah's I think," [30]

Evelyn comments, "The angels and heaven have been using the original system all along and now we are going to need to learn it."

Sean says, "How hard can it be?

Evelyn replies, "Well the angels will be back in a few, shemonim, you can ask them why there are now only 18 hours, O, I'm sorry, I mean, mawnahs, in a day."

Sean says, "Touché", then he hesitates for a moment, then looks at everyone at the table, "Did that really happen last night? Did the earth actually sing praises to God? Did the entire sky fill with angels, singing for hours the praises of God? Did the Spirit and glory of God flow over us like a river, through us and into us?"

By the time Sean finished his question, everyone at the table with tears flowing down they're cheeks, said, "Yes, we were there, it was all real, we all saw it, we all felt it."

Sean continues, "After all the years that I despised him, made fun of him, belittled him, now this? He loves me? He has forgiven me. Last night I slept like a baby for the first time in my life, total peace in my heart all my stress is gone, it's like I can breathe with a full breath."

Sally, weeping, says, "He still here, can't you feel him? His presence, his love, his Holiness and Spirit."

Then they hear the shofar blow to alert the people that they will be leaving soon. The crew spends a few moments drying their eyes and getting their composure back. Then proceed to get their packs, which contain the few things they will need during their trek. They carry only some water, food (lunch and snacks) and some personal items, like their new combs and writing pads, the journals.

They follow the tribes out of the camp, going west. As they move about two miles along, they come to the crest of a mild hill. As the tribes begin going down the other side of the hill, they can see for the first time what the land looks like now. The land is empty, nothing there, no buildings no fences, no roads. The road that they came to Petra on should be there somewhere, but they can't find it.

Then Laura says, "There it is, but it doesn't have a surface on it, it looks like it's been scrubbed away."

While the crew is marveling at how complete the cleansing has been, Sally says, "What is that?"

They look and see dust being raised just behind a hill to their right, north. They can't tell what is causing it. They think, maybe it's an army.

Sally says, "Where are the angels when you need them?"

Then she hears a voice right behind her, "Sally", the voice says, "I'm right here."

The angel proceeds to explain, "This dust is from the wild animals of this area. We had sequestered them into safe locations, paddocks, and roosts for their protection during the battle. We had been feeding and watering them for the past 3 weeks in the desert."

The angel pauses then continues, "The animals were brought to the edge of the camp last night to hear the praise, and to participate."

Evelyn asks, "How can they participate?"

He explains, "The animals had lost their ability to speak in a language at the time of Adam's fall in the garden, it was part of the curse from God, for their part in Eves deception. [31] Last night when the Holy Spirit flowed out on everyone, he went to the animals and restored their tongues, now they can speak again. Six thousand years they have been waiting for the restoration to come. The miracle is done.

They will be travelling along, adjacent with you, as we go to Jerusalem. The earth cannot support the animals at this time, in fact it cannot support man either. It will be years before the earth can support life."

Then the angel adds. "Don't let their presence bother you; they have been reconciled to each other and to man. They do not eat each other anymore; they will not threaten you. The wolf can now lay down with the lamb, and the lamb is not afraid."

Evelyn says, "I'm not afraid of them, I just had no idea that the animals could talk at some point in the past. Why didn't I know?"

The angel replies, "In the 20th century the Bible had been relegated to a book of myths by most people. Had you read it; you would have known."

The angel continues, "There is an account in scripture where the angel of the lord opens the mouth of an ass, so he, the ass, could have a heated discussion with his owner, a man named Balaam."

Evelyn asks again, "Does this mean that the relationship between animals and people has changed?"

The angel. "It will make it easier for you to know if an animal is sick, or tired, or angry, without violence. Communication is a good thing for all concerned. However, the kingdom structure which gave man dominion over the animals, has not changed, a child can lead them, but it should be a much smoother relationship than before."

Isaac has been listening, and says, "cool".

After walking about four hours, the tribes are given a break for lunch and rest. Sean estimates that they have travelled about eight miles. He figures this is actually good considering the children and the older people.

Sean says, "This will be about 12-15 miles a day."

The angel says, "We hope that it will get better as we go, the people will get stronger as they go, there are healings taking place and the air is getting thicker down in the rift."

Sean responds, "Healings? What do you mean?"

The angel continues, "Human afflictions and diseases are caused by stress, the environment, spiritual attacks and genetics. The spiritual attacks are gone, the demons are judged, your environment is good, your stress will continue to attenuate, and God is healing your genetics. Most of the people you see here today, including you, will live to be well over one hundred and fifty years old."

Laura turns to Sally and asks, "What did he say? Did he say we might live to be one hundred and fifty years old?"

Sally, "Yes he did, but there must be a translation problem here, no one can really live to be that old."

The angel continues, "This is a new world, the old corrupt world has been erased, purged, the tempter your adversary the devil is bound and [32] incarcerated in Sheol. Your aging process will be greatly slowed down, your children who are born in the kingdom after this time, could live almost a thousand years. This is the future God is offering you and the others." [33]

The crew is stunned, they go silent, each contemplating what the angel said, they just walk along the way without a word.

After what seems like hours, Isaac turns to Sean, "You know These desert clothes that we're wearing are really comfortable. At first I felt weird in them but I'm getting used to them now."

Sean nodded in the affirmative and then added, "These open shoes actually work well, they stay much cooler and are in the shade of the clothes."

Isaac, "I've never been a sandals guy, it must be an English thing. But these really do a good job. It is a new world after all, I need to adapt."

The tribes and crew had reached the western end of the Petra road and had turned north about two hours earlier. For the crew this is uncharted territory. They had come to Petra from the south three weeks earlier. As they move along the east side of the rift valley, old Jordan, they can make out some sort of structure in the distance. It looks like a small tower. It appears that they are travelling towards it.

After another half hour of travel, they can now tell that it is indeed a tower and it is sitting in an encampment just like the one they left this morning.

One of the angels appears and begins to explain, "This is your camp for the night."

Sean asks, "Did you move our camp to this location in front of us?"

The angel, "No, your camp from last night is being moved to tomorrow night's camp location. This camp is a duplicate of the first except for the tower."

Isaac chimes in, "Is it a watch tower? Is there something you need to watch for?"

The angel, "No, it's for you and the tribes. We have found that people like to get a view of where they've been and where they're going. And you may like to see the assortment of animals travelling with you. Over in the paddocks to the east."

Laura steps forward and asks, "You could have transported us to Jerusalem, could you not?"

"Yes", the angel says.

She continues, "Then why are you making us walk? Why can't you carry us there?"

He explains, "We angels are servants of the living God, we do exactly what we are directed to do, we do not improvise or change things. When we are given a schedule, we follow it precisely. We know that God knows what needs to be done and why, he is infinite in wisdom and understanding, we are not."

The angel continues, "That does not mean that we are always in the dark as to why and how. God knows that we are curious and like answers, so he generally shows us his purposes, but he does not have to."

One of the other angels arrives and says, "The Holy Spirit, has explained some things to me. First, he says, Laura, the walk will do you good."

The angel pauses, then continues, "You will have more time to acclimate to things and there are sites to see, before reaching Jerusalem.

Also, you attached yourselves to the tribes in Petra and they need to walk, in fact they want to walk, up to Jerusalem. Record the trip in your journal, make the most of it."

The angel says, "One more thing, I'm to tell you, that you and the others should begin asking the Holy Spirit when you have questions."

Laura looking perplexed says, "This is all so new and different to me, I'm not sure I'll ever understand."

The angel replies softly, "Laura, all truly meaningful relationships require time to develop, be patient everything will be fine."

Isaac asks, "Why do the tribes what to walk to Jerusalem? It seems to me they would like to get home as quickly as possible."

The first angel replies, "They know that their old homes are all gone, the Jerusalem they left years ago is gone, everything except the temple. They know that they're going to start over, but they are excited to be going home just like their ancestors did thousands of years ago, using the same path, they also see the significance and continuity of the events."

Isaac says, "Amazing, after all this time it's still all about family."

They all continue into the camp and find their quarters in the same locations. They can't wait to get off their feet, close their eyes and relax. Just before they start to get up to go the mess hall, two angels came and sat down with them at the table near their compartments.

One of them says, "We told you we would let you know today, if any of us will tell our names to you. Well we discussed it, and two of us are willing to tell you our names."

He continues, "My name is Ya'atiel, and his name, as he points to the other angel, is Boaziel."

Laura asks, "Do your names have meanings?"

Ya'atiel replies yes, "My name means "God's guide" or "a guide from God", and Boaziel means "a pillar in God's house".

Sean stands up and says, "Thank you both for trusting us with your names, we are honored."

Isaac asks, "You two look really rested and strong, especially since you sang for hours last night and travelled all day with us."

Boaziel replies, "Actually we stopped the praise service after just two hours, for you and the camp. We continued to worship by ourselves nearly all night, we are not frail at all, we are the mighty Gibbor, the mighty ones. We even reduce our appearance, our size, so we don't intimidate others."

After dinner Isaac and Evelyn stroll past the tower on the east side of the camp, they see a long line of people waiting for an opportunity to climb the tower, they just look at each other and Evelyn says, "maybe tomorrow". By the time they get to they're quarters the others have already turned in for the night, Isaac says "see you in the morning".

In the morning Isaac comes out of his compartment and finds Sean already at the table having breakfast and reading something. Isaac laughed and said "I guess I won't need to wake you today; did you not sleep so well?"

Sean replies, "No, actually I slept great! I had asked the Lord to wake me early in the morning so I could better prepare for the day, and he did, he woke me, and here I am."

Isaac asks, "So what are you reading?"

He replies, "It's a time chart, so I can cross reference the hours verses mawnahs, the new time units., a mawnah is 80 shemonim (minutes) long and there are 18 mawnahs to a day. At the equinox there are 9 mawnahs in the day and 9 mawnahs in the night, every 30 days the sunrise and sunset will change by 1 mawnah, either shorter or longer depending on the season, summer or winter. The 24-hour days have no such relationship." [34]

Sean continues, "This chart also covers the new, actually the old calendar, that the new world will be using, it shows how the weeks of days, and weeks of weeks, or Jubilees work. The chart is round, and has several different wheels which can be rotated to give answers, I haven't seen one of these kind of charts in years, it works great and there are no batteries to run down. There's a chart on the table for each of us to have."

Isaac asks, "have you been told about the calendar, the 364-day solar calendar?"

Sean, "Yes, but only that it exists and will be used in the kingdom." Ya'atiel says we'll discuss it tonight."

Isaac, "cool".

Sitting around the table the whole crew discuss how well they all seem to have recovered from yesterday's trek. The crew finishes breakfast and goes to the assembly point.

The morning seemed to go by in a flash, and they're talking about how many animals are in the herds just to the east of them, there seems to be more than yesterday. The birds that are travelling along with the animals, are flying around in great flocks, flying in circles and making loops. There are more different types than you can imagine, each species trying do more than the others, it's like a great aerial show, no one chasing anyone, they're all just celebrating the new kingdom, just having fun.

After lunch and their afternoon trek, the crew sees their camp, a welcome sight. They also realize that they had not seen the angels since they left in the morning.

Sean turns to Isaac and says, "I'm looking forward to talking to Ya'atiel about the calendar tonight."

As the crew finish their dinner, and are sitting around writing in their journals and commenting on how they now understand the need for daily foot washing, Boaziel comes walking up and gets the crews attention. He says, "Stay in your chairs don't get up."

He continues, "Many of the animals in the paddocks have expressed curiosity about your camp and people in general, they have asked if they could walk through and see what you're like. Many of these animals have never seen a person up close or seen your dwellings, we have told them that we would escort them through the camp and back. They have agreed to just follow us, they will be coming past you in about 15 shemonim, do not laugh or make comments, they understand more than you think." [35]

Laura turns to Sally and says, "Is he serious?"

Sally, "I think so."

Isaac just says, "cool".

Sure enough, they see the animals coming along the roadway between the dwellings. There are four angels clearing the way in front and setting the pace, within the animals are angels walking with them, every so often the angels stop and point at things and talk to the animals, they are explaining and answering questions.

Evelyn says under her breath, "I've noticed that some of the them are sniffing around, this is like a petting zoo, in reverse. I think I've seen it all, a parade of talking animals being led by angels." The whole crew reaches for their journals.

Then Sean notices that Ya'atiel is in the middle of a group of ibexes, long horned mountain goats, explaining things to them, Sean can't help but smile, he thinks to himself, *"I get to talk to him when you're done"*.

As Ya'atiel passes by the crews' location he makes eye contact with Sean and says, "Tomorrow, okay?" Sean nods back and smiles.

As it seems that all the animals have past their location, there is a short break, and then they see them, the cats, not just a few but more like a hundred. They are grouping themselves by types, lions, leopards, tigers, and jaguars, they fill the area from side to side. They are moving slower than the other animals were.

Laura whispers, "I know we're not on their diets any more, but look at those eyes, it's un-nerving, there is nothing between us and them, I hope they don't forget."

About half of them had passed by, when one of the younger lions brushed up against one of the people watching, it was just like what a house cat would do, but the person was nearly pushed down. Then a deep voice came from the middle of the cats, "stop that!", everybody looked towards the voice, it was the biggest lion of the group, the young lion quickly slipped back into the middle of the group, all was well.

The parade takes a mawnaw or 80 shemonim (minutes) to pass their location and three mawnaws to complete the full tour.

Two days later, and 30 miles further along, the crew sits at the morning breakfast table. Isaac asks Sean if he got to talk to Ya'atiel about the calendar.

Sean replies, "Yes, it all boils down to sevens, seven days to a week, the days are not named only numbered, except day seven is also called Shabbat. You can have weeks of days or weeks of years, seven years is a year-week, if you multiply a year-week times seven, you will have a jubilee, which equals forty-nine years, a jubilee. The next year, or the fiftieth year is called the year of jubilee. Dates are designated by year, 1-7 and year-weeks, 1-49, a jubilee, today is in year one, of week one, of jubilee one, this would read 1/1/1.

Years are still tracked but not for dating purposes, just for festivals and planting cycles. There are still twelve months per year, with four Thirty-one-day months and eight thirty-day months, the months are not named, only numbered. So today is the 4th day of week 1 of month 1 of year 1. This would read 4/1/1, If you need to have a complete date from day to jubilee, you can add the week-year number (1-49) and then the jubilee number. This would read 4/1/1/1/1, or the fourth day of the first jubilee."

He continues, "This calendar was originally given to the prophet Enoch before the flood, and then abandoned by the Israelites when they went to Babylon and Assyria. Enoch's calendar was established long before any of the gentile nations made their own calendars. The gentiles replaced God's calendar with their own, they wanted to honor their own gods."

Sally says, "I understand that the Tribes in Petra had a hard time accepting that their Jewish lunar calendar is not acceptable."

Sean, "Yes, however Boaziel says that Moses, was informed by the angels, that his people would start using a lunar calendar, and that this calendar, because of its complexity, they would lose track of the actual date, and be in error. It was for this reason no one could predict the dates of the jubilees accurately." Sally pauses, looking perplexed. [36]

Evelyn says, "I'm looking forward to the trek today, Boaziel told me to look at the dead sea when we get there. He did not tell me why, just to look."

The shofar blows and the crew begins to move. They don't know it, but they are walking on the old dead sea road, which follows the east bank.

It only takes about two mawnaws for them to see the southern extreme of the sea. But they are confused, they thought that the southern portion was being mined for minerals and salt. But now the mineral ponds which crossed the sea are gone. They reason among themselves that the mining works would be destroyed just like everything else, so no big surprise.

As they continued watching the sea Sally exclaims "It's moving, the water is moving, can't you see it's moving".

Everybody just looked and said what's moving? Sally says, "The shore line."

Sean, say's, "She's right it's moving south."

When the tribes stopped for lunch and a rest time, the crew were able to see that the front edge of the sea to the south was indeed moving, flowing. It was fast enough that the crew could track its progress.

As they watched the angel Boaziel walked up to them, and told them, "The southern edge of the sea is ten miles further south than it was earlier, and the separation between the northern, and southern parts of the sea are completely gone, completely under water. If you look closely at the western shore directly across the sea, you can see a river entering the sea."

He continues, "The river is an ancient one which had not flowed for thousands of years."

As the crew look, they can see it clearly, it's not just a creek, but rather is a large raging river coming down from the canyons above.

Boaziel continues, "That river is at Zohar, and there are four more, even larger rivers flowing into the sea, the others are further north, the Tse'elim, En-eglain, En-gedi and Mitspe Shalem, all on the west bank, the sea will rise seven hundred feet above its old level. There is a large amount of water flowing literally from under the temple foundations in Jerusalem flowing east through a new gash in the mount of olives, which guides the water to the dead sea. The dead sea will become capable of sustaining life, the dead sea will be dead no longer. The earth quake that you felt just after Jesus left Petra, was caused by him when he came down on the mount of olives, just east of the temple mount. Causing fissures all along the west side of the rift valley, releasing massive underground reservoirs." [37]

Isaac asks Boaziel, "Can the water reach up to our location,"

He responds, "Yes it will. It will go hundreds of feet over this old road bed that you are walking on, but don't worry we will be gone before it gets here."

The tribes stand up and begin to move forward, Isaac says, "It's time to move along, let's go." Everyone smiles.

Three Mawnaws later they are looking at the main body of the northern dead sea. They can clearly see the rivers flowing into the sea. The one coming down from En-Gedi is the largest.

The angel Boaziel points out, "Do you all see the flat area up on the bank next to the river, that point is where the old village of En-Gedi used to be, it's located seven hundred feet above the old dead sea level. That village will be rebuilt and used as a sea port in the future. People will fish from that location." [38]

The trek continues, and comes to this night's encampment. They can see that it has a tower.

Sean says, "Maybe we can watch the sea from there to night. Once we're there we'll have to hurry to get up there. Maybe even put dinner off for a while."

Let's do it."

As the crew enters the camp, they decide to climb the tower first thing, in hopes of getting in front of the crowd. Laura and Evelyn decide to go on to their rooms, but Sally stays with Sean and Isaac.

As they finally reach the top of the tower, they move quickly to the western edge to look out. As they begin to identify locations and rivers etc.

Sally sighs and says, "I wish I had my camera and the telescopic lens; I could take some marvelous pictures from here." Then she hears a voice behind her say, "Sally, don't look back, only look to your future."

Sally thinks, that's not one of the angels, who is that, then she hesitates, could it be? She turns to look, and there is Gus!

She exclaims, "Oh Gus, it's you!"

He steps forward and gives her a big bear hug, she whispers into his ear, "I've missed you."

He responds, "I've missed you too."

Isaac chimes in, "Hey, where is my hug?"

Gus looks at Isaac with that look, and then says "I wouldn't want to hurt you."

They all laugh and shake hands. Sean ask's Gus, "What do you think of the sea, isn't this amazing?"

Gus responds, "Yes, I was in Jerusalem just this morning and got to see the temple site. The water is coming directly from underneath the temple foundation, it is at the top of the hill, yet the water is under pressure. It is a river and flowing into the sea through the old mount of olives, I'm glad to see this end of the river also. [39]

The topography of the whole Jerusalem area has been altered. The saints are there and are working like crazy to get things ready for us, to come up, we'll be camping in the area north of the temple. What used to be called southern Samaria, or more recently the west bank."

Sally asks, "How far is Jerusalem away?"

Gus, "We should be above the Jericho plain tomorrow somewhere near Anata, after the trek. The next day, we will all gather at the temple site. The ceremonies will continue until they are complete."

Sally, "What ceremonies?"

Gus, "I can't say much about them, it's not my place, but I do know that we, the six of us, will be together in a location up close, up close to the Lord."

Isaac asks, "How do you know that?"

Gus, "The Lord told me, I asked him and he told me."

Sally asks, "What, you talked to Jesus?

Gus, "Yes, it is part of my job, Oh Sally, you just wait, he's amazing!"

The crowd on top of the tower is growing, so they turn and start down the tower,

Isaac notices that Gus is not dressed like they are. He asks, "How did you get out of wearing clothes like ours".

Gus just smiles and says, "Do you like them?"

Isaac, "Yes,"

Gus, "So do I." His smile turns to a grin as he walked on.

The next day just before lunch the tribes come to the side of the river Jordan, just north of the dead sea. It's clear that the dead sea is filling to the north as well as the south. The water is backing up in the river bed filling out to the east and west.

The news crew is still at the back of the tribes and can't see the water or shore line.

Sally says, "This is where the original tribes used the ark of the covenant to stop the water, and cross on dry land."

Sean looks at Sally and says, "You've been studying? Do you think it will happen like that today?"

The others just shrug and say "Who knows."

Then Gus says, "I don't think so, I saw a bridge there yesterday, when I was up above in Jerusalem."

Isaac asks, "You could see the bridge from Jerusalem?"

Gus, "Yes the bridge is a long, military style temporary floating bridge. It is easily seen from 12 miles away at the top of the ridge. The bridge has to go over the end of the sea at its current level, which is rising all the time."

Gus is right, they all walk over the bridge, it is at least a mile and a half long, and thirty feet wide. It had been finished just days ago, just for this event.

A bridge will be built in the future to cross the river further north somewhere near the old town of Beit She'an.

Gus says, "I think this bridge was built in the third heaven and brought through in pieces and erected here."

The tribes continue to climb up out of the great rift valley and they come into a large open area near the hill tops. It is the site of the ancient village of Anata, Anata is no more, the tribes camp is set up here. There is a lot of spiritual activity up at the top of the hill, angels in, angels out, and lights shining into the air.

As the people begin to settle in to their rooms, they are particularly tired and sore, this leg of the journey was very grueling. Yet for all this there is still a level of excitement within the camp, tomorrow Jerusalem!

Sally asks Gus, "Where is the city?" He says, "The city is gone, the preparation is for the temple enclosure." Gus stops and points, "It's just over that hill, Sally, try and get some sleep."

CHAPTER FIVE

Jerusalem

As the sun breaks over the mount of olives, in the east, it seems that everyone in the camp is not just beginning to stir, but are up, dressed, and working on eating their breakfast. This day is not just another day, everyone expects to hear and see Jesus today. Jerusalem is just over the hill.

The people had been told last night to wash themselves and wear the new clean clothes that have been provided within their rooms by the angels. Everyone complies, and it seems that each tribe have different clothes to wear, each tribe has unique colors and patterns on their garments. And the angels are sorting them out by tribe. The tribes are ordered by the birth order of the twelve sons of Jacob. Everyone within the tribes is going to the ceremony, this means husbands, wives and children, no one is to be left in the camp.

The 144 thousand Jews were here in Jerusalem just three-and one-half years ago, when Jesus came down on the mount and sealed them with the father's name in their foreheads. They were told to flee to the wilderness for refuge, now they've come full circle, back to Jerusalem.

The news crew and the other gentiles within the camp have been following the tribes all the way from Petra, but today they are told that they will go up first, this not because of any honor but rather because of their seating location in the congregation, on the temple court.

As they came over the ridge of the hill, they were between the mount of Olives to their south and the mount Scopus on the north, in a saddle between the hills. They could see the temple just below them. The temple was setting just west of the old eastern wall of the temple enclosure. They could see that the eastern gate which had been closed by the Muslims, was now open. It had been used at the Lords return. The area around the outside of the gate was cleansed also. The crew could hear the tribes shouting and praising God when they saw the city and the gate.

Sean mentions to Gus, "When the tribes first heard that Jerusalem was razed, they were heart broken, but the angels explained that the Jerusalem that they knew and loved was almost all Islamic and crusader, not David's city at all. The Jerusalem that will be built on the site will be God's."

Everyone could see the waters issuing out from under the temples eastern and southern foundations. It was very impressive and the whole procession stopped momentarily when they saw it. The temple itself was not very big and not particularly impressive, there are no buildings around it, it stood alone.

As they begin to broaden their view of the temple enclosure, they realize that the original eastern wall was only a small portion of the full eastern wall. The rest of the wall, including the other three walls are all new. They've been built since the Lords return.

The new enclosure is massive, Gus estimates that it is at least one-mile square. To put it in perspective, the enclosure covers the entire old city, from Golgatha in the north, all of the City of David in the south and well past the mount of Zion in the west. The entire area within the walls is leveled to be just below the temple foundations, the temple foundation is approximately 15 hundred feet square, and will be further west than the existing little temple. [40]

The modern Jerusalem which was outside the old city, which existed when the 144 thousand Jew's left Jerusalem three- and one-half years ago, has been completely razed to the ground. It's clear that the Lord is starting over.

Sally looks toward the south end of the enclosure and sees what looks like an encampment, similar to their camp.

She asks Gus, "What is that, or who is that?"

Gus says, "That camp is for the worlds refugees which survived the antichrists marking system and death squads. They were not Christians. I think that there is about two hundred thousand of them. They were extracted from all over the world before the Lord destroyed the nations. I watched it happen."

As the procession moves along, they can see what looks like a sea of chairs behind the back, western side of the temple.

Again, Sally asks Gus, "Who are the chairs for?"

He replies, "They are for all the tribes, the refugees, and for us. Anyone who cannot stand all day. There are temporary latrines as well, and water stations. The amazing part is that everyone else who is attending can stand and go all day, angels and the saints of God will fill this entire area."

The procession comes to a new gate in the new northern portion of the eastern wall. As they come near to it, they realize that its larger than they thought, the wall is three stories high and the top of the gate structure is above that. The gate can accommodate large loads and traffic in both directions. There is a causeway leading up to the gate from the outside.

They enter the temple mount platform, the one-mile square enclosure. According to the Biblical book of Ezekiel this site is five hundred reeds by five hundred reeds square, and that everything inside of it is holy. It is technically part of the temple and has an area three time greater than the old walled city of Jerusalem.

They proceed to the west end of the temple; it is over a quarter mile walk. There they see that there is a raised platform on the west end. The angels lead the crew and those with them to chairs on the left of the platform, the south side. There were about five thousand gentiles in Petra along with the tribes.

Just like Gus had said, the crew was seated in the second row, on the inside on the aisle, right up front. The others were filing past them and being seated. Gus was looking back towards the rear of the area to see the refugees.

He says, "I have strong emotional ties with these people, I watched them one by one being delivered from certain death. They were going to be killed by the beast's followers, but the Lord would pluck them up and bring them out, and now here they are!"

The refugees were being seated behind the Petra gentiles, in a fan shape towards the center of the area. The 12 sealed tribes were being seated directly in front of the platform at the temple.

Sally was sitting next to Gus, as she heard someone call, "Audee-el, Audee-el."

She turns to look and sees an angel coming directly towards her. She thinks to herself, *"I don't know this angel."* But as he gets closer, she can tell that he is actually looking at Gus, not her.

She whispers to Gus, "Why is he saying Audee-el?"

Gus, "Because that's my name, my kingdom name, Jesus gave it to me."

Sally, "Why didn't you tell me?"

Gus, "I had not found the right time, but I was going to."

When the angel reaches Gus, he says, "Peace be unto you, I'm going to be your interpreter, not just you but the whole news crew."

He turns to the rest of the crew and acknowledges them, they return it, with a nod.

The angel proceeds, "The primary purpose of the ceremonies today is to bring the entire kingdom together at one time, and to bring the newcomers under the scepter, the Lord's rod of authority. Each person will bow the knee and head before the Lord himself, and acknowledge him as their Lord and sovereign, or not. The Lord will accept or reject the candidate. They will be called by name, and the candidate will back away with the head down, and turn to your left and go to a new seat on the right of the platform. This procedure is going to take a long time to get done, so be patient, and remember the longer it takes the more people are entering the kingdom, rejoice with them."

Laura asks, "The Lord may reject a candidate?"

The angel responds, "Yes, he knows the heart, and knows if someone is lying to him. It is, of course best to tell the truth."

Evelyn asks, "Will there be other ceremonies in other countries around the world for people who can't be here today? To bring them under the scepter?"

The angel, "No, there are no other people in the world, these are the only ones that did not take the mark of the beast and managed to hide and survive. This is the only ceremony."

It was apparent from the blank look on the crews faces that it has finally sunk in that the world is gone.

As they sat there in the seats, they heard the shofar blow. It was a strange sensation, they could see that many shofars were blowing at one time, but the note was as if it were one horn, a single pitch as only one shofar. It blew without stopping for at least a minute. When it stopped everyone in the seats dropped their heads and bowed from the waist.

After a moment of silence, a booming voice says, "All rise, behold the Lamb of God which taketh away the sins of the world, who gave his own life as a perfect sacrifice for sin, and has redeemed us all unto God!"

And then as if from nowhere Jesus is standing directly in front of the throne on the platform, or more precisely the altar.

The voice continues, "The kingdoms of this world are become the kingdom of God and of his Christ!"

This time the people gave a great cheer and began to shout, "Holy, Holy, Holy, Lord God almighty, which was, and is, and is forever!"

The Lord stopped the praise after just moments, and said, "I honor my Father and the Holy Spirit."

He then sat down on his throne and nodded to someone on his right.

The angel interpreter tells the crew, "You should face Jesus, then bow the knee and head, and then say, you are my Lord and Sovereign", Jesus will say rise, if he has something to say to you, it will be at this time. Regardless you will need to back away and turn to your left and exit under the Scepter to the Lord's right." [41]

The crew all acknowledge the angel, and take a deep breath. The first row of people, are already up and moving toward the Altar.

The angel says, "Let's go."

As they moved forward, the first person went under the Scepter, the tribes in front of the altar began to sing and praise, the ones closest to the front began to dance before the Lord. Just as the tribes started singing, the skies above and around the temple site were full of the Saints of God, The resurrected church of Jesus Christ, his bride. They all began to sing and shout and praise God, there are millions.

Laura follows the other members of the news crew, as one by one they bow and pass under the scepter, she sees each of them listen to Jesus and speak back to him, she thinks to herself, *"For the first time in my life I don't know what to say."* She's in front of Jesus, steps forward and bows the knee and head, and says "You are my Lord and Sovereign". She hears Jesus say, "Laura," she looks up and he says, "Laura your grandmother is here today, and would like to see you." Laura says, "who?"

He continued, "When your grandmother heard that you were in Petra, she rejoiced for you."

Jesus leans forward and gently touches her forehead, instantly she sees a memory of herself as a very young child, being held by her grandmother, a memory so old as to be one of her very earliest. Her grandmother was weeping, and praying for her.

Jesus continues, "Laura, be at peace, I've made all the arrangements."

Then she heard a voice saying, "Laura, come this way." Two of the saints were guiding her to the Lords Rod, and she goes under and continues to her new seat. After she sits for a few moments she realizes that the news team had been set in the reverse order, and that she is in the second seat from the aisle, and Gus is not with them.

She asks, "Where is Gus?"

Sally, who is sitting on Laura's right, responds, "He is still on the platform, he asked the Lord if he could remain there to watch the refugees pass under the Rod. Gus really cares for them!"

Sally continues, "Jesus just pointed to a spot near the scepter, and said "It is yours," it seems that everyone around the Lord knew that it was his, there was no confusion at all."

As Laura is turned right and listening to Sally, she feels that someone has sat down next to her, on her left, in the aisle seat. She turns to look, and there is an attractive woman setting there. She's looking at Laura.

Laura, looking back, locks eyes with the woman, then Laura melts as she perceives that see is looking into the eyes of her grandmother. Oh, what eyes they are!

Laura reaches cautiously with her hand and touches her, and whispers, "Your real. You're not a spirit, you're real! I haven't touched anyone since we came to Petra, I was afraid to, because I thought that it all could be my imagination, not real."

Her grandmother responds, "Yes I'm real, and so are you. Oh, Laura, the memories just flood back into my mind. In heaven, we are so excited to look forward, to the things we get to see and do, that the old life simply fades away. When I first heard that you were in Petra, I said, Oh, Lord let it be true. Only moments later Jesus himself confirmed the report and said, "she is safe." I thought to myself, *"Oh. If I can only see her."* The Lord replied, "You can, be patient."

Laura comments, "I can't believe you are alive after all this time."

Grandmother explains, "Laura, in Jesus no one dies, you, me, all of us here today will live forever, we have eternal life, it is the free gift of God!"

Laura hugs her grandmother, places her head on her shoulder and they watch the ceremonies together. Laura realizes that the day is simply beautiful, it is still early morning and the sun is still rising from the east.

People are continuously passing under the scepter. It becomes obvious that Laura is not the only one to have family connections in God's kingdom. She sees saints, men and women, greeting their children. The children often look much older than the parents.

Laura comments, "I'm not sure if I'll ever get used to the age thing, you know, the saints don't age."

Grandmother comments, "You will get used to it, Laura are you hungry? Come with me, let's get something to eat."

Laura responds, "Can we do that?"

She says, "Yes of course, come with me."

They go to a location north west of the congregation, where there are dining tents set up with tables and chairs. They get some food and drinks and sit down.

Laura's grandmother asks, "Tell me your story, how did you get to Petra?"

Laura says, "Oh my, that's a long story."

Grandmother, "That's okay we have all day."

It's been most of the day and the ceremonies continue on. The angel comes to the news crew and tells them that they will be required to go to their camp in about one half mawnah, (40 shemonim). The ceremonies will end soon and the Lord wants everyone home before shabbat, sun down. Their camp for tonight is located near the refugee camp near the southern end of the temple court, the one-mile square enclosure.

The news crew finds their rooms in the now familiar location within the camp and they begin to relax at the table out front. They are all there except Laura, and they are beginning to be concerned that she is going to be late.

But, just shemonim from sundown Laura and her grandmother come walking up. Everyone is relieved, Laura seems very relaxed. Laura informs the others that her grandmother will be staying with her for the shabbat, she introduces everyone to her grandmother and they all sit down and begin to talk.

Grandmother says, "I feel like I know you all, Laura has spent the afternoon sharing your story, and how you made it to Petra.

First of all, thank you for being such good friends to my granddaughter, she loves you all.

Second, I hope you all realize how blessed you are to have been removed from the judgement of the world, billions were lost, and only you and the refugees remain. If the Lord had not cut short the events of the end, no one would have survived. The mystery of iniquity was nearly full, the world was completely overcome by sin."

Gus says, "Yes I know, I watched the Lord extract the refugees right out of the battle field, right before they would have been killed."

Grandmother asks, "You actually saw them?"

Gus, "Yes I was a witness."

"Oh, that explains it, you're Audee-el, one of the fifteen witnesses. What an honor to be mentioned in the scriptures."

Sean asks Laura's grandmother, "Where do you think we will go from here?"

She replies, "I can't be very specific but I can give the general process, understanding that the earth is cut and bruised and not capable of supporting people or the animals living on it right now. The earth, waters and atmosphere all need time to heal, different areas need different kinds of assistance. The air and the waters will recover quicker than the earth itself. The earth will be allowed to remain fallow for a long time, it will recover naturally, the trees and grass will grow undisturbed. The areas that suffered atomic warfare will be the worst affected, and the longest to recover, the Lord has already started the purification from the radiation, this is in conjunction with the removal of all the blood."

Laura asks, "Grandmother, you won't get in trouble for telling us these things, will you?"

Grandmother, "no, no I won't, I'm approved to tell you what I know. I don't know all the details; I don't need to know the details." Then she said, "Ya'atiel, would you like to join us?"

Then from the open area in front of the rooms, Ya'atiel comes walking up, and says to her, "Continue, I'll support you if needed."

She thanks him and continues, "While the earth is recovering, your needs and the needs of the animals will be supplied by the angels and saints. The saints have been making, and will continue fixing the meals for everyone on earth, there are millions of Saints that desire to contribute to your welfare. The supplies are in heaven, the third heavens. Everything you need, but you cannot produce will be provided. During this recovery time, your jobs will be to help build homes, buildings and fences. All of the infrastructure which can be built without rehabilitating the land."

Sally says, "I've never built anything in my life."

Grandmother smiles and continues, "Relax, all the jobs will be suitable for your abilities and talents. You will all continue living in the temporary shelters your using now, until homes can be made available.

Don't think that manual labor and jobs is all you will ever do, when you receive your homes you will also get locations for orchards, olive trees, fields for wheat and corn and vineyards. Once your inheritance is up and operating, you and your neighbors will have time to expand your horizons, things you cannot even imagine will be available to you and your families, we'll talk about those things some other day."

Isaac asks, "things like what? for example."

She laughs, "Like, travelling beyond the vail, and like seeing and understanding things, you don't even know exist! The bible calls it the hidden manna." [42]

Ya'atiel says, "You have been living with the Hebrew tribes, but soon you will be moved to be with the refugees. The tribes have their inheritance here in Jerusalem and the land of Israel, and they will camp right here where they are. Their homes will be built outside the city of Jerusalem.

The Lord will reign from this temple enclosure, and David will be the governor over Jerusalem, the city and the new nation of Israel, he will reign from his new palace somewhere in the city."

Sally asks, "David? Do you mean the real king David?"

Ya'atiel responds, "Yes, he was promised by God, thousands of years ago, and God does not forget promises." [64]

He continued, "The refugees are currently being sorted out by their family associations. And will be grouped into their own tribes and given areas for their inheritance. Many smaller families will need to join with other families to make their tribes large enough to be viable for the future. The starting locations of the new settlements will vary based on the original home lands of the tribes, the people will start near to us here and migrate to their final homes based on the needs of the populations. The tribes will grow much quicker than the earth of the past. The lack of sickness and the ease of child birth will help very much. The lack of stress, and knowing that everything you need, will be provided to you, will lend itself to rapid population increases. Longevity will also affect the number of generations each generation will produce. The world will be totally self-sufficient within the first jubilee, forty-nine years, there will be over five million gentiles alone."

The news crew just sits and stares at each other, They are obviously over whelmed, what a day, the ceremonies, the Lord, and information about the future, has them in total sensory overload, it's going to take some time to process it all.

Grandmother says, "While understanding what to expect, and how events may play out is important to you, remember that you are now living in a world that has no more war, no more hunger, no more horrific weather events, not even earthquakes. It is a special world for you and your children to be a part of. Rejoice that sin and iniquity cannot flourish anymore.

I suggest that you keep things simple and take one day at a time. I also suggest that we all call it a day and get some sleep, before Laura turns into a pumpkin."

Then Laura laughed and said, "Oh, grandma! You do remember."

Laura continues, "When I was a young girl I would try and stay up at night, too late, and I would get grumpy or lose control of my emotions. When grandma would see it coming on, she would say, your turning into a pumpkin, I would understand and go to bed."

Grandma smiles at the memories and says, "The angels and resurrected saints are far more robust than people, and we forget how much stress you are going through. This is all good stress, no negative events at all, but still it requires a lot of mental energy to process what has happened. May God's peace cover you and give you rest."

Evelyn opens her eyes, and sees that there is sun light coming into her room. She instantly thinks to herself, *"Why did I not her the shofar? What's wrong?"* Then she remembers it's shabbat, and she relaxes a bit. As she begins to get dressed and comb her hair, she hears a knock on her door, it's a polite tapping not at all demanding. When Evelyn opens the door, it's Sally, she asks' "may I come in?" Evelyn lets her in and ask's "are you okay?"

Sally responds, "Yes I'm fine. I woke up a little while ago and went outside, it was so peaceful and quiet that it seemed unreal, then I realized that the whole world was sleeping in the temple enclosure and there was total peace. And of all the people on the earth, no one had anything they had to do today, nothing had to be done, everyone was at rest, there are no guards to protect us from ourselves. I started to weep with joy and I just had to tell the Lord, thank you, thank you Lord. "Then she tells Evelyn, I guess you would have had to have been there."

A short time later the news crew and also Laura's grandmother are sitting around outside enjoying the morning. Laura asks her grandmother, "What are the rules for the shabbat?"

Grandmother says, "I will try and keep this simple and straight forward, understand that the Lord had finished the creation in just six days, six 24-hour days, after he finished creating, he desisted and reposed on the seventh day, he reflected on the world and all he had done. His reaction to his world was, IT'S VERY GOOD. The actual Hebrew word for: 'rested', is 'shabbat' and means to repose, and desist. God did not stop because he was tired or because the angels could not go on, but he stopped because he was finished. The Lord sanctified the seventh day and observed that day every week. He first allowed two classes of angels, the angels of presence and the angels of sanctification to observe the shabbat with him in heaven, then later with Moses on the top of mount Horeb, God opened the shabbat to Jacob and his children, through the

Levitical system. No one else, no other people were allowed to observe shabbat. The gentiles were not included. [43]

When Jesus fulfilled the Levitical requirement for a perfect sacrifice, he did not extend the shabbat blessing to the gentile converts, Christians were not required to observe the shabbat. They were also not restricted from observing shabbat if they desired, it was a free choice, most Christians honored God on the first day of the week."

She continues, "Jesus still observes shabbat. While the bride, the saints, still have a free will, thus can chose how they can spend their time, I think that the saints follow the Lord and do whatever he wants. Revelations Chapter fourteen says, 'They follow him whither he goeth'. We are after all his bride."

"You and the other refugees are Christian's and have the option to observe or not. Not following the Lords lead seems odd to us but, everyone has the choice.

The shabbat is a day off from work, I don't know why anyone would hesitate to participate. I think that the Jews in the past had turned it into a legalistic burden, which was hard to bear. The rules put in place by God for shabbat were there to keep the dishonest from cheating. People want to get a head start on the next week by starting a little early, or working just a bit more than his neighbor by getting something done on the shabbat. The shabbat was made for man, not man for the shabbat. God stopped and looked at his creation, which included Adam. He did not create Adam to look at his creation with him. Jesus fulfilled the law when he went to the cross and removed the Levitical system, and replaced it with grace and mercy."

Grandmother turns to Laura and says, "Laura, let's go for a walk over to the temple and see the waters flowing out. I will be leaving in the morning to go back to my life in heaven, and I don't know how long it will be before we can talk again."

Laura stops and asks, "Don't we have an eternity to get things done? Can't we spend more time together?"

Grandma laughs, "Nice try young lady! But I have places to go, people to see, and things to get done. I don't want to miss them. Most of my activities and work will be done in the third heavens, however understand that if I can work it out, I'll see you when I can." Laura just says, "Okay, it's that I only just got you back and now your leaving." They turn and begin to stroll away towards the temple, arm in arm.

CHAPTER SIX

The First Jubilee

Sean is gazing out over his fields and groves, from his roof top patio on his home. Laura comes up the stairs from down below, and asks, "Well are we going?"

Sean ignores his wife's question and say's, "I'm still amazed at how much progress has been made in just one jubilee. Look at the trees and fields, the prosperity that God has given us. The angels and even your grandmother thought that it would take longer for the world to recover than it has. We get multiple harvests every year and the fruit are larger and sweeter than anything from before the kingdom."

Laura responds, "Don't you ignore me Mr. Wright."

Sean again ignored her and continues, "I did not think that all of this progress could be accomplished without modern equipment and plows and chemicals, but it has, the earth yields herself to us, and we receive the blessing. We do use the horses and oxen, but almost as much for their happiness as for our needs. The animals need to feel needed and we can help them."

Sean says, "You know Mrs. Wright, I used to hear farmers say that the dirt gets into your blood, and you can't get it out. Now I know what they mean, I've never been so satisfied."

Turning to Laura, he smiles and says, "Yes, we're going".

Laura asks, "How many of us?"

Sean replies, "As many as wants to go can go. I think that some of the grand kids would get excited about taking a pilgrimage to Jerusalem. And I think they need to see the temple, the Lord and angels."

Laura asks, "Have you forgotten that it's one hundred and fifty miles south of us here, and what about the little ones, the great grandchildren, you know we have a dozen."

Sean, "The grandchildren will be fine, and I talked to Audee-el a while back and he offered to provide transportation for you and I and the little ones."

Laura exclaims, "Oh no you don't! I'm not getting into one of those chariots of fire. I'd rather walk. And, I'm not sure that I what my children in one either."

Sean laughs, "You've never hesitated to get into jet planes and travel around the world, spending hours in the air."

Laura smiles and comments, "I wasn't eighty years old back then."

Two weeks later, Sean whispers to Laura, "We're here."

Laura say's "You're kidding, we just took off." She looks around and indeed they are at the temple mount, the Ophan, is gently landing, the new temple is beautiful and much larger than the old little temple structure that was there fifty years earlier.

As they unload and begin to organize the little ones, and move away from the Ophanim that they realize how full the court is.

Laura says, "We should have come earlier to get a good location."

Sean gestures for Laura to follow him, he starts to a location near the front left of the platform area, and as they near the front they see the others. Their children, and the grandchildren. The grandchildren come running to see Laura, but her kids don't even turn around, they're talking to someone. As Laura gets closer, she gasps, "Oh, grandma!" Laura's children are talking to Grandmother.

The children had heard about the scepter ceremony and how grandmother had come from heaven to see Laura, but it was just a story to them, now it is real, grandmother is a real person, no myth here. Laura goes to her grandmother and there are hugs all around. The children, now old enough to have grandchildren themselves, are the first generation of the new kingdom, they look at Sean and Laura with apologies in their eyes, they acknowledge that they had their doubts. They thought that it was a bed time story, designed to give them good thoughts.

Sean says, "All the stories that we have told you about our past, and things we went through are true, we would never lie to you. Never let anyone tell you different."

Sean notices that Sally and Isaac are in the seats adjacent to them. They are married and have two generations of children with them also.

Everyone thought that Gus and Sally might get married, but it turns out that Gus was more like a big brother, and he had decided to put off any plans for getting remarried anyway.

When Isaac asked Sally to marry him, she said, "cool". Isaac told Sally, "When you were hugged by Gus up on the tower, down by the Dead Sea, and I asked, where is my hug? I wasn't asking Gus; I was asking you."

Laura asked Sally, "How did we get seats next to each other?"

Sally responds, "All of the people from Petra were given seats together here tonight. The angels are acknowledging our presence at the original first day concert and worship service."

Laura asks, "So where is Evelyn? Shouldn't she be here?"

Sally, "She's here, somewhere back over in that area behind us. Her husband has family back there, and she's with him not us. We're going to try and talk to her tomorrow morning before we leave. We are also hoping to go over the hill and see the Dead Sea, Isaac would like to see the beach at En-Gedi."

Laura looks at her adult children talking to her grandmother, and she whispers to Sally, "Can you believe how taken my kids are with her?"

Sally says, "Yes I can, their universe just got bigger, there is a heaven, spirit realm, and most of all, there is life after death. You can tell them that it is true, but until they know it for themselves, it's not real. Just wait till they see Jesus and a sky full of angels, I can't wait!"

They all settle down and wait for the celebration to begin. Laura says, "Sally do you realize that we don't need an angel interpreter any more. None of us here today speak anything but Hebrew. Even Sean and I don't speak English to each other. Sometimes I still dream in English, but not often."

Sally replies, "English seems foreign to me now, I've really moved on. My kids speak Hebrew even better than I do."

Sally turns her head and looks at the platform area behind the temple, and says, "Did you hear that? I think it's time." Suddenly the shofars blow, loud and long. And then a great voice, that says "Bow the knee," then announces that "The Lord of Lords and King of Kings is before you! Behold the Lamb of God, who takes away the sins of the earth, praise him!"

There appears a host of angels on the platform all the way across it. Their wings fully out stretched and transfigured and from the center of the host comes the Lord Jesus, he steps forward stops and begins to pray over the congregation.

"I am the Alpha and the Omega, I am he that liveth, and was dead, and behold I am alive for evermore! I honor and glorify my father in heaven!"

The Lord continued, "Behold I stand at the door and knock, if anyone hear my voice, and open the doors of his heart, I will come into them and they will be my children. Bring me the children."

The Lord sits on a throne near the front of the platform, and the Saints, his bride begin to bring children from the congregation to him.

As they come, the leader of the angelic choir, the Morning stars, shouts to the congregation, "Were you there when we sang praises to God on that first day, fifty years ago!" and the congregation exclaims, "Yes, yes, we were there, praise be to God!" The angelic choir and orchestra began to sing and praise God. The Morning Stars in full numbers begin lifting up God, and the skies are full of angels, what a marvelous site. The congregation shouts, praises to God and joins in to the songs.

The Saints of God are going through the congregation inviting and helping parents bring their children to be blessed by Jesus. They take Sally's and Laura's family to Jesus. Laura and grandmother and Sally watch from the edge of the platform as each of their offspring are personally introduced to Jesus.

The praise and worship continue all evening, what a night! As the younger children are coming back from their appointments with the Lord, they are taken back to the booths which are set up on the edges of the temple site. These are the same encampments which were originally used by the people when they came to Jerusalem, They have remained in service for the people who come each year for the feast of tabernacles, as required by the Lord, [44] tonight they are being used by the members of the congregation, who are not from the Jerusalem area.

69

The spirit of God rests over the temple and enclosure, peace settles down and the night begins.

Laura hears Sean whisper, "Laura, wake up, it's morning and we have visitors, get dressed and come on out."

As Laura comes out of the booth, she sees the news crew sitting at the table outside. All six members are there, with hot drinks and blankets around their shoulders, she smiles and takes her place at the table.

Evelyn, looking kind of sheepish says, "I have something that I need to tell you all. Last night after we all went to sleep; the Holy Spirit came to me and gave me a list of instructions to give to each of you. The instructions are very specific and must be followed precisely. First, you remember the journals we were told to keep the day we left Petra? Well the Lord wants you to translate your original comments from English to Hebrew, don't change anything on the original journal. Also make a side by side, line by line Hebrew and English copy of everything in the journal. Each of you are to do this for your own journal, if you need translation help you can ask Thomas Taylor for help, you can ask Gus to contact Thomas for you. Gus you were not there, you were with the Lord, so you do not have a journal."

She continues, "Each of you are to make a list of everything you left behind in Petra, be as accurate as possible, everything from combs to video cameras, every piece of equipment you had to leave behind should be on the list. You must also make a list of operating instructions for each item, as if it is for a novice to understand, tell them what the equipment was designed to do and how to trouble shoot any problem. Explain your hand operated battery chargers, which are designed for field use. Show how the equipment can be linked together and are related to each other. Be sure to include all of your computer passwords and special commands."

Sally ask's, "What is this all about?"

Evelyn shushes her and say's in English, "Let me continue. Make a description and a map for the stone chamber in Petra which we left all of our possessions. Make it as accurate as possible, try to remember as many details as you can, about its location. Remember how it was not with the other chambers because we came later than the Jews."

She continues: "Start the tasks right away don't put it off, when the journals are complete and ready, make a compiled book of all five journals and maps and lists. Give a full compiled book to each crew member for safe keeping until the end of the age. Tell no one what is in the book, not even your neighbors, don't take it out and read it to the family, hide it within your belongings. It should be kept by your families first born, and only he will know what it is and what it says. You can trust angels and saints but no Enoshe."

As she finishes, she says, "Souls are at risk."

The other members don't know what to say, so they all just drop their heads and begin to pray, "Lord help us to be obedient to your will, guide us, strengthen us, and give us wisdom…"

CHAPTER SEVEN

Yahweh University

Isaac comes walking into his farmhouse, located about 150 miles north of Jerusalem, and calls to Sally, "Guess what? Oh, never mind, you could never guess this in a million years!"

Sally sighs, "Now what."

Isaac continues, "When we first started reading Thomas Taylor's research books, back in Oklahoma? Well, remember how he had written about the saints of God, those who were devout and overcomers during their lives, would be blessed in heaven with the hidden manna from God." [42]

Sally replies, "Yes I do, it is from the book of Revelation the second chapter, I think. The term 'manna' in Hebrew means 'what is it?' So, God would reveal the answers to hidden questions."

Isaac sits down on a kitchen chair and leans on the table, and says, "Do you remember the last time we were in Jerusalem, how we saw those big buildings that were built on mount Scopus, just north of the temple area."

"Yes, of course."

Isaac, "They were finished about fifteen years ago and have been open for the saints of God. They are called 'Yahweh University' and the Saints go there to take classes in hidden manna, how cool is that!"

Sally says, "I think that the classes are only available to the saints, the ones who were resurrected. The refugees are not accepted, that's you and me.

Isaac, "Actually I was talking to Thomas Taylor earlier and he said that some of the classes will be available to the refugees of the scepter ceremony. Basically, anyone who went under the scepter. The deep spiritual classes are limited to certain saints, but some classes are more historic, and the refugee believers can participate.

Sally, replies, "Where were you that you saw Thomas? He's assigned to Jerusalem."

Isaac, "Actually, he came up to me, while I was out in the barn. He said, that when he heard that the classes would be made available, he thought of us. He came straight here, and brought some application forms for us to use, and even some suggestions on how to fill them out."

Sally asks, "Did Thomas leave?"

Isaac, "I just asked him if I could come in and tell you? And he said yes."

As Isaac was talking, a knock was heard at the back door, and Isaac jumped up and opened it, sure enough it is Thomas.

Sally calls to Thomas, "Come in, please come in! Isaac is so excited that he forgot you were in the barn, I'm so sorry." Then she gives Isaac that look.

Thomas just smiled and said, "It's okay, I know Isaac, that's why I came. But. I also came to tell you as well."

Sally asked, "Thomas how much does it cost to attend a class?"

Thomas, "Nothing, God does not sell blessings, all the blessings of God are gifts. All of the Lords gifts are free. He wants you to understand him, and how he operates. What he does and does not do. He always makes decisions based on the good of his kingdom and his subjects.

If your application is approved, he will have made a place for you, not just in the class, but also to provide food and lodging in Jerusalem as the class is in session. He also will provide you with transportation to and from Jerusalem."

Thomas continues, "The first class which is available to you, is called 'Abraham's ten trials'. [45] Each trial requires a day in class and a day on site. The angels which protected, guided and taught Abraham during his trials will come and speak to the class, also Abraham, Sara, Isaac and others who were actually there, will add to the revelations being presented.

God can transcend time, and place you in the locations of the past as the event is taking place, you will be able to see the spirit activity and entities working behind the scene. God's angel instructors, will point out things of interest as they happen. This is not a re-enactment or holographic projection; it is a time entry.

In the Bible, prophets would be taken by God and shown future events in real time, as they were happening. [46] In this class it is the same, except you will be going back in time not forward. Eventually you will be shown classes about the future as well."

Thomas stops and asks Isaac, "Do you think that you two would be interested in taking the class?" And then he adds "Don't over think this."

Sally replies, "Do you really think that we could be accepted to take the class?"

Thomas, "God never overrides your personal will, your right to say, no. You don't have to take the class if you don't what to, the choice is yours."

Thomas continues: "Actually I know for a fact that you are already approved, it was the Lords idea, that you two be offered the class, I asked him if I could present it to you and he said yes.

You will still need to fill out the forms, but if you decide to take the class it will be in the twentieth day of portal five, basically one month from today.

I took the class two months ago and it was really amazing."

Isaac and Sally just look at each other and nod to the affirmative.

Thomas pulls up a chair to the table, lays out the applications, and say's,

"This won't take very long, let's get it done."

One month later, Isaac and Sally are walking towards the campus of Yahweh University, on the old hill that was called Scopus. Scopus was a medical university before the war, and was destroyed by the Lord during the purge, the day of the Lord. The area is now used almost exclusively by the saints. There are at least a dozen new large multi-story buildings, some are for class rooms and some are for student housing.

Isaac tells Sally, "I've never seen so many happy people, not phony happiness, but legitimately happy people! They greet and converse with total ease."

Sally says, "Why wouldn't they be happy, that which they believed for, in faith, is happening right in front of them, and it's better than they could ever dream.

It is like you and I, having the time of our lives, we're strolling hand in hand through Jerusalem, taking in the sites."

Isaac and Sally have found their dorm room and are relaxing on a balcony, they have found a class list on a table in the room and are looking at the topics available. They are amazed at the sheer number of classes listed.

Sally says, "Look at some of these classes;

'קריאייטיב לוגואים' 'creative Logos' it has 4 progressions,

'הבנת המציאות', '*understanding reality*' it has 5 progressions, 'צייתנות והרצון', '*obedience and the will*', it has 7 progressions, 'מבצעי האמונה', '*the operations of faith*,' it has 4 progressions, 'קדושה ויצירה', '*holiness and creation*,' it has 6 progressions."

Isaac shakes his head and sighs, "Did you see, there are 35 pages of classes available to the saints, and I don't even understand what some of them mean. Maybe we are in over our heads?"

Sally says, "No, I don't think so, Thomas said the it was the Lord's idea, and I think he knows us, and what we need. We need to trust God."

Isaac agrees, "Your right, it's just that there is so much to learn."

He continues, "How do you think they light this room? There are no lighting fixtures, no light bulbs, it seems as though the light comes from the walls themselves. There is a one-inch square patch on the wall with an arrow pointing up and another patch with an arrow pointing down, they are used for controlling the light level. When we were brought into the room the lights appeared to come on and rise automatically, the saint that was showing us how to use the lights told us to just leave them on dim when we leave the room, and not to try to turn them off, because it is not manual."

Sally laughs, "Weren't we told that the entire universe is 99.99% energy, with little or no matter? So why should it surprise us that the walls can light themselves, they are just energy. I do think, that the controls are amazing."

She continues, "It's the windows and walls that surprised me, you touch a button, and a window appears in a solid wall! The beautiful stone block wall, transforms into a window and you can even make it bigger or smaller, or tint it as desired, all this with the patch panel by the bed."

Isaac says, "I was glad to see that at least, they still use doorknobs to operate the doors, and we can still go outside on the balcony."

The next morning after breakfast, they find the classroom and go in. They are surprised to see that it is not very large, about forty feet across and it is round. Around the outside there are twelve seats and work stations, in the center there are some tables, chairs and control panels and book shelves. There are scrolls, books and papyrus documents scattered around on the tables.

There is room for about ten people in the center of the room, and a corridor to the back wall, where there is a faculty entrance door, which is opposite the student entrance into the room. There are also charts and pictures somehow displayed in the back wall and domed ceiling of the room.

There are people filing in, they are shown where to sit by a saint working at the school. Sally and Isaac are shown to their seats, and to their surprise they are not next to each other, there are several seats between them. They can't help but wonder, why they were separated.

Sally works up the courage to ask, "Why can't we sit together?"

The helper looked surprised, and then answered, "Oh, with your husband?

It's not that you can't sit together, but rather that there is an optimum location within the class for you, and that's where you are. I forgot that you and your husband are Enoshe. In the kingdom of God, you are seen as individuals. You and your husband are the first Enoshe to enroll in a class here, and this is new to us."

Sally asks again, "There seems to be only room for twelve students in the class, is there a lack of interest?"

The helper responds, "No, it's has nothing to do with interest, none of the classes at the university have more than twelve seats, The Lord wants everyone to feel like they are very important, and are able to see everyone's face up close and personal, the class is intended to be an experience."

When Sally finishes her inquiry, she sits down and looks at some of the devices that are on the desk, and a woman comes into the room from the instructor's door, and sits on a chair near Sally's location.

Sally thinks, *"Who is this lady? She is a very beautiful woman."*

The woman turns, looks at Sally, and smiles. She asks, "Are you Sally?"

And Sally says, "Yes, and your name is?

She says, "It's Sarah, Abraham was my husband, Isaac is my son and Jacob my grandson." Then she points to a woman who had just walked into the class and say's, "That is Emzara, she is our grandmother, Noah's wife and mother of the three brothers from whom we are all descended." [47]

Before Sally could respond, the class is called to order, she just leans towards Sarah and say's "Thank you, very much".

An angel starts the class with a prayer and blessing. And tells the students that he is the angel of presence that had spoken to Abraham at the time of the sacrifice of Isaac, when Abraham was told to stand down and not hurt the child. He will facilitate most of the class.

And then he begins to tell any first-time students that the hand held devices which are provided on their desk are for their use in the class and they can be taken back to the dorm room for use in the evening.

He continues by introducing the other members of the faculty and guests. He starts from the oldest to the youngest. The group is like a whos' who of the book of Genesis, Noah was the first and his wife Emzara with him.

Noah starts explaining the conditions of the world from just before the flood came, and washed it clean.

He only touches briefly on the lawless ones, the Nephilim, giants, and all of the sins and the uncleanness they represent. He does talk about the vexation of the spirits of the Nephilim on his children during the early days after the flood.

He still has a hint of regret in his voice when he speaks about how quickly his children began to forget the lessons of the preflood world. He explains how he had lived a total of eight hundred and fifty years as an Enoshe and how he had to witness the sins and spiritual decline of his sons for three hundred and fifty years after the flood.

But his countenance picks up when he recalls his grandson, Abram, "Abram was born two hundred and ninety years after the flood, through the linage of Shem, my first born, Abram was my tenth generation after the flood, I knew Abram for fifty-eight years during my life-time."

He continues, "I spoke Hebrew when I came out of the ark and we all lost our ability to speak it, when God confounded the languages at the demise of the peoples' tower of arrogance. [48] But God allowed Abram, to learn the language of creation again, because Abram returned to the old ways of God and forsook the demons and idols." [49]

Noah turns to a young man sitting several seats away and say's "This is my son Abraham", and then looks to a young man seated next to him, and says "My first-born son Shem", and then sets down.

Shem stands up, and says, "I am Shem Bet-Noah, I lived both before and after the great flood, I saw the grace and power of God." He continued to explain that he lived one hundred years before the flood and five hundred years after the flood, and that he saw Abraham born, and the day of his death. Abraham is the tenth generation after my father Noah.

"I was given the land that Canaan the son of my uncle Ham had usurped from me, the land that we are in at this very time,(now known as Israel) it was given to me by God, and revealed by the drawing of lots with my father Noah, only thirty two years after the flood. Abraham, by divine right already owned the land of Canaan before he went to it, it was his all along. Abraham never demanded that the Canaanites or any one else be removed from the land. He only sought for a place to live with his family, a city whose builder and maker is God."

He looks up, takes a deep breath and says, "I want to make it clear that in having this class about Abraham and his trials, we, his family do not wish that any honor or undue respect be given to our lives or decisions, as though we were special. Our lives only appear to be special because of the grace and power of God made manifest through our lives, God chose us to receive and display his blessing for the other nations to see, we were just fallen men, just like all mankind. We thank God and glorify him for his mercies and love to us and you, praise be to the risen savior, our Lord Jesus Christ. We were the first fruits of resurrection, when Jesus came to us in Sheol and called us to go home to our father in heaven." Then Shem sat down.

The angel of presence moves forward and introduces Sarah, Lot, Isaac, Jacob and finally Terah, Abraham's father. Each of them gave some information concerning Abraham and their relationship with him. One thing that runs through all of their comments and memories, is that they are a close and loving family. Regardless of their own short comings and mistakes they all really care for each other.

Terah, Abrahams father winds up his comments by listing the ten trials of Abraham. He calls the first two trials as trials of country. [50] Abram had to leave his home in Ur of Chaldees and go to Haran, and then, the second move from Haran to Canaan. He had left his home not knowing where he was going, I told him to send for me, if things worked out.

The third trial is called, "A trial of famine," Abram has to go to Egypt.

The fourth trial was, "The battle to recover Lot," Lot is the son of Abrams brother Haran, Haran had died in Ur of Chaldees and Abram had adopted Lot, he was like a son to Abram. Lot had chosen to go to the plains below to live, down in the valley east of Hebron, He lived in Sodom, Sodom had been attacked by the Edomites and others, and everyone in Sodom was taken away as slaves. Abram went with his armed servants and recovered them. Lot did not return to Abraham's home, he stayed in Sodom.

The fifth trial was, "The wealth of kings," Abraham was offered the wealth of Sodom, all that the king had, for a reward in delivering the city. But Abram refused to take anything.

The sixth trial, "When Abram's wife had been torn away from him in Egypt."

The seventh trial, "When God required Abraham to circumcise everyone in his family and servants."

The eighth trial, "When Abraham was told to send Hagar and Ishmael away into the wilderness."

The ninth trial, "God's command that Abraham sacrifice his son Isaac."

The tenth and final trial was, "Abraham's request for a burial place for Sarah his wife, in the two caves of Mamre."

When the list was finished, Terah, Abrahams father, set down and the angel of presence stands up. He allows the class to mingle amongst themselves and also talk to Noah and his family. The ease at which these people, the ancient saints, and student saints are able to communicate with each other, really amazes Sally and Isaac. They don't seem to have anything to prove to each other, they are all friends and friendly to each other. Sally and Isaac are accepted and embraced just like everyone else.

After the class, Isaac and Sally go to eat and then go home to their dorm, they realize that they are beat, really tired, not physically but mentally drained. They sit on the balcony and marvel at the reality of having talked to the most famous people that have ever lived, and that they were very human, they are just like us, and they love God and are devoted to their savior, the Lord Jesus. Abraham marveled at the price and sacrifice that Jesus payed at calvary.

Some of the other students, saints, are from the twentieth century, but some were from hundreds of years earlier and their bodies were resurrected from the catacombs in Rome. The class has quite a mixture of saints, from different locations and times.

Something that became obvious to Sally was that the saints are much more robust than she and Isaac are. When the saints were resurrected, they were changed, not just spiritually and intellectually, but also physically. They are not just very smart, but they need less rest, and they go much longer without sleep, and they eat less. They can jump further and higher and lift more. Being resurrected really is something to be looked forward to. [51]

Isaac is excited about tomorrows class, because the class will do a time insertion back to Abrahams time. He tells Sally, "Let's get some rest, I'm worn out."

Sally says "Go ahead, I'm going to use the remote device that we were given at the class, so we can review everything we covered in the class, and access the libraries held here in the university." Isaac just says, "Be my guest."

As Sally and Isaac enter the classroom the next morning, they find that all the students are already there.

Isaac asks Sally, "Are we late?"

Sally says, "No, we are actually early, I think everyone is very excited to go back in time."

After a few moments the angel of presence calls the class to order. He explains that Abraham and his family do not participate in the time insertions, they don't like seeing themselves as they used to be, especially over and over, every time there is a class. So, their participation is limited to the class room studies.

The angel also explains that there will be a rather large group of angels travelling with them today, to assist you, should there be any problems. There is no problem with time insertion or with us being there, but sometimes the environment can be overwhelming.

He continues, "No one, save God and his angels have ever gone back thru time. There have been some Enoshe that have moved forward through time, but not back, Enoch, Daniel and John, to name a few. There are others that you would not know, because they were not recorded in the scriptures. These prophets which moved in time had some issues, mostly emotional.

We have found from the numerous classes we have already conducted in the past fifteen years that resurrected saints are better able to handle themselves. The saints are already used to travelling, in and out of the spirit realm, and they work with spirits and angels while they are there. However, there are still some newer saints that get queasy in the spirit, and still can experience some fear.

We have two Enoshe in our class today, Isaac and his wife Sally. They will be the first non-resurrected to be time inserted. Their ability to handle the experience will allow the class to be opened to other Enoshe in the future."

Isaac whispers to Sally, "No pressure here."

The angel hears Isaac and echoes back, "No, that's right, no pressure, we feel you and Sally will do just fine. My discloser is more of a formality. You and Sally will travel with an Ophan, to the location, which today will be Ur of Chaldees, the saints can travel on their own. He then gave everyone their coordinate to meet at, and say's please go straight there, we are on a schedule." Then the whole class began to laugh.

Sally and Isaac felt the warmth around them and see the shield covering them, the Ophan says, you can hold each other if you wish. They then feel the ophan lift up, then take off like lightning. In seconds they are at the site and being released, what a ride! They actually arrive slightly before most of the Saints and angels.

The location is near a river, the Euphrates, there are no building or land marks there, only young trees and grass. Then suddenly they feel a pulse of energy pass through them, they feel different somehow, and there are a group of angels standing around them.

Isaac says, "Cool,"

One of the angels, the one directly in front of them and facing them smiles, and say's. "Yes, it's cool."

Then the angels in front of them begin to step away and to the side, Isaac and Sally can see that they are standing in a small town of mud brick buildings and there are people walking right past them in the street, and there are people sitting in the street around stone fire pits, cooking and working. They cannot see Sally and Isaac.

Isaac is impressed with the general operation of the city going on all around him, but there was a buzzing sound that he could not understand, then he saw them, spirits, demons floating all around the people and their activities. The spirits could not directly touch anyone, but they were talking to them and shooting past their heads. They were trying to distract the people with their antics. Some of the people had several spirits sitting on their shoulders and speaking directly into their ears and thoughts, they would point at something or someone else, and the person would turn and look in that direction also. It was obvious that the spirits were communicating with the people.

Sally said, "Don't listen to them, don't listen to them."

The class walked further along and came to a structure full of idols, and they were packed into the pavilion thousands upon thousands of spirits, more like a bee hive. There was a young man there with his father, that young man is Abram, when he was just fourteen years old, he pointed out to his father that the idols could not help the people, and that we should turn to Yahweh for our help. His father agreed that the idols and spirits were worthless but that the people really liked them, and won't let them go. Abram protested to his father, they are false gods they mislead and deceive. [52]

The angel walking with the class says, "The ratio between men and spirits was very bad for people, at this time in the world, the spirits came through the flood in the millions, but the Enoshe only had eight souls. Even after three hundred years there is still a gross imbalance, the people are still being overwhelmed." [53]

The angel continues, "All of the spirits you seen here today were arrested when the Lord returned to set up his kingdom. They are incarcerated in the pit with their fathers, and are now waiting for their judgement."

The angel asked for everyone to close their eyes, and then when he confirmed that they were all closed he said open them. When they did, they found that it was now late night time, but the class was still at the house of idols. They could see that there is an older Abram, Abram proceeds to light the building on fire and escape down the back street. The building is engulfed in moments and quickly burns. The class watches as some of the people come to the aid of the spirits to put out the fire. The class watches as at least one of the fire fighters is overcome and killed by the flames.

The angel says, "This event was the reason Abram and his father had to leave Ur. One of the fire fighters that was killed was Abram's brother Haran, Abram in his zeal had inadvertently killed his own brother." [54]

The angel says, "It's time to leave, close your eyes, then the pulse that send them back in time, passed through them again, and when they opened their eyes they are back in real time, and the ophan is waiting for Sally and Isaac.

Sally asks the ophan, "How long did you have to wait?"

He says, "About four shemonim, that would be four minutes to you." He takes them back to the class room.

When they are back in the class room, they are asked by the angel of presence how they felt about the experience, especially the spirits and demons.

Isaac says, "I had only seen spirits from a distance, back in Petra, but never so close. However, I never felt threatened or afraid, you had told us that we were out of their reach. Also, that we would be a threat to them, had they actually known we were there."

Sally responds, "The spirits made me angry, I hated their tactics and lies, I'm so glad they've been taken away and can't hurt anyone anymore."

The angel asks, "And what about Abram?"

Isaac continues, "I feel that I know and understand Abraham much better now, and how hard it must be concerning his brother. I understand why he would not want to be time inserted, and see that event again."

Sally says, "He is a tremendous man of convictions, he saw how false the Idols were." Isaac inserts, "I'm looking forward to the next class."

The angel replies, "Good, so are we."

CHAPTER EIGHT

A Rod of Iron

Sean is watching his boys bailing hay in the field north of the house. The fields closest to the house are for produce and herbs, and the next fields are for vines and fruit trees, and then the field for grain and animal forage are beyond.

As Sean watches the progress, he hears a voice from behind him, say, "Hello Sean." It's the voice of an old friend, whom he hasn't heard for some time, probably fifty years. Sean smiles to himself, and turns to see him, its Gus, or more properly Audee-El.

Gus, has a large open grin on his face, and they shake hands and hug each other. The boys stop what they are doing and just stare at the two men, who is this, that just walks up and hugs our father?

When they say father, they could mean anything from grandfather, to great, great grandfather. Sean has three generations of grandsons working in that field today. He has four generations of offspring at this time, and he has hundreds of farms from here to the north, fanning out from the original homestead. Each of his sons receives an allocation of land, tools and animals, when he turns twenty years old, they can farm the land themselves, with their own children or they can combine it with one of their brothers and work it together.

As the family increases in size some of the children are choosing to go into the trades, to make clothing, shoes, farming implements or whatever their gifts might be. Because there are no armies or militias, the sons don't have to learn how to fight in an army or make weapons. There are some of the sons who perform the duties of law enforcement. The crime rate is very low, almost non-existent. Nearly all disagreements are handled within the family. There are small groups of local police offices handling misdemeanors and small disputes.

Sean invites Gus back to the house, and as they walk along Sean asks, "so, Gus are you on a social call or is it official?"

Gus laughs, "That's a fair question, since I haven't come to see you for fifty years. As it is, I'm in the area on official business, but not here to see you on official work."

Sean says, "We've heard that you have risen to one of the top positions in the Enoshe law enforcement offices."

Gus, "Yes, I'm now in charge of the northern districts, from the northern border of Israel, all the way to the northern frontier. There are several colonies further north than you are, they started their farms nearly five-hundred miles further north, and they are growing almost twice as fast as your family. We figure that it is because they were from remote tribal areas when they were delivered from Bet Sharrukin, they understand the need for a large family. They just don't seem to understand that the infant mortality rate is not like it was before the war. They also seem to have a difficult time understanding that the Lord can hear every word they say, indeed, he can even hear every thought."

They come to Sean's house and go up the outside steps to the roof top deck, Sean calls Laura to come up and see Gus, Laura shouts back, "Gus, who? We don't know anyone named Gus, the only Gus we know, never writes, never calls, never comes by to see us, it can't be that Gus!"

Gus says, "I deserve that."

Laura asks Gus, "Can you stay for dinner tonight?"

Gus consents, and Laura goes down stairs and gets dinner started.

Sean asks Gus how his family is doing? Gus was not married at the first jubilee ceremonies, he married just a few years after that jubilee.

Gus married a widow woman named Vera, who was in the refugees. Her husband had been killed by Bet Sharrukin's troops during the overflow campaign in western Russia, She and her two young infant sons hid out, deep in the forest for over four years. The sons now have several generations of children themselves and are living in a settlement on the northern frontier. Gus and Vera, live in Jerusalem and split time with another home in the north.

Gus says, "It's just Vera and I at home. It's kind of nice being able to get close to some one again. We can be ourselves and talk very openly to each other. It is so much better than my first marriage from before the war. That relationship just went from one conflict to another."

Sean says, "When we, the news crew, were getting ready to leave Petra and walk to Jerusalem, one of the angels told us that we would probably live to be over one-hundred and fifty years old. I remember thinking, that he was crazy and exaggerating. But now, sitting here with you, you're over one-hundred and fifty years old, and don't look a day over sixty, I realize that he was probably being conservative."

Sean continues, "I think back to how it was before Petra, and how perpetually stressed I was, I realize that stress was really killing me. Then I was filled with the Holy Spirit that night when the Morning Stars sang, and everything changed."

Gus says, "I understand Sean, for me the stress went way down when the temptations abated. I could not believe the rate of the temptations that were being placed into my mind, until they stopped, and I only had to deal with my own thoughts, and not every dart that was shot into my mind by the spirits.

None of our children born here, after the war, have ever heard a temptation from the spirit realm, they are only tempted by other people or animals, and they know who is talking to them, and they reject it so much easier, and it shows. These children today have so much more victory in there faces, so much more life."

Sean comments, "You still have to be very direct with each and every one of the children, they must know the truth, everything about the past and the future, it's not easy, because you don't want to be negative, but they must know. Most of our children born during this age are going to live all the way through to the end. They will be there when Lucifer is released to deceive the nations. it's hard to understand how it could come to that."

Gus, "Sean, your children trust you, and know that you love them and would not lie to them, but our generation is the last direct link for mankind back to the world before the war. We can say from experience exactly what was happening back then. But when we are gone, our testimony can be questioned, others will question our motives and honesty. Some will say that our memories are clouded and not at all accurate. It is similar to Noah and the flood, His children reverted back to the doctrine of the demons, as soon as Noah and Shem died, the flood became a myth."

Sean concurs and continues, "I can see that the equipment and data storage from our time in Petra is full of research sources and historic information that we had with us before the war, the sources cannot be questioned like us, it would be like a smoking gun."

Laura arrives with the food, thanks is given, and everyone starts eating. Laura asks, "Gus, can you explain to us, what you think the Lord means by the term, 'rod of iron'. We hear from people in our area, that God is going to rule with a rod of iron. Sean and I don't see it, we don't feel ruled at all, but our neighbors feel like there is going to be a crackdown on everybody at some point in the near future."

Gus responds, "It means that the discipline of God to his people, is stiff, and unbending, like a rod of iron. In the courts of man before the war, Armageddon, it was difficult to be 100% certain, that the person was guilty, or what his motives were. The accused person only had to prove a reasonable doubt, and show that he might not be guilty. Thus, the guilty might be acquitted and released. This can never happen now, in God's kingdom, no one can get away with crime, or sin, because the Lord knows.

The Lord knows that mankind, the Enoshe, are not happy when they feel that they have no privacy. He goes to great length to avoid disrupting their lives by feeling too close to them. But the Lord sees all, hears all, understands all, even the thoughts of the heart, he cannot deny what he knows and cannot pretend that it did not happen, all transgressions of his laws must be judged and a judgment made.

The laws during our time right now are the same as before the war, 'the wages of sin is death' and the means for mitigating the effects are the same, it can only happen through the shed blood of the sacrifice. The shed blood of Jesus himself on the cross. If a person denies their actions, claims ignorance or pleads insanity, they will be shown the truth and judged accordingly."

Laura asks Gus, "Why does he need you? Could he not simply remove offenders himself, and get it over with?"

Gus nods, "You're right, he does not need me, he could do it himself, however he chose not to do that, he prefers to have Enoshe deal with Enoshe. The scriptures say that all men have sinned, and fallen short of God's standards, I would be judged just like everyone else and no one else would survive the judgment. It is not God's desire to judge everyone, but rather to change us, and make us into a new man able to choose righteousness and live accordingly. One of God's personal attributes is longsuffering, he gives a person time to exercise their free will to choose life and to desire change."

Sean asks Gus, "How does the justice system work right now, and how do you fit in?"

Gus laughs, and says' "Well, first of all my part is very straight forward. But I should start with the heavenly law, a law written down in the books in heaven. This law requires that all angels, and now heavenly saints, must inform God if they ever see anyone, angel or man, transgress God's law, at any level. None of the angels or saints can see something happen and then turn a blind eye to it, it must be reported. This law is a means to check on the honesty and fidelity of the heavenly host. It was probably this law that discovered iniquity in Satan's heart. Scripture says that God found iniquity within thee. [55]

Nearly all the requests for investigation to my office come through angels or saints, they very seldom take action themselves, aside from protecting the innocent at a crime. A complaint comes to me and all the information and direct evidence for my investigation and subsequent legal actions. Sometimes we inform the person that is offending, that we are aware of his actions, and he needs to repent and confess his transgressions to God and ask for forgiveness, if they do it, all is forgiven and his record is cleared. The sad part is, that we have never had a complaint that was not true. The Lord wants the Enoshe to govern their own lives at the personal and civic level, on serious matters the Lord himself can be the one that judges the case and gives the sentence.

The idea that you, Laura, don't feel ruled by pressure from law enforcement sources, simply means that you and Sean are dealing with any mistakes, or bad choices, as soon as they happen and allowing the Lord to wash them away. It also means that you are not fighting with your neighbors, which is where the real crimes usually get started. It is a great compliment to your family, that I have received no complaints of requests for investigation, pertaining to you or your family."

Laura says, "Thank you Gus, we are trying to do our best. By the time we get through eating it will be dark, we would like you to stay with us tonight."

Gus, smiles and says, "Thank you, not everyone wants me to stay at their home. I need to be up front with you, I am sometimes called in the night to respond to unpredictable events, if that should happen don't let it bother you."

Sean's first-born son, named Adam and Adam's first-born son John, came to the house when they heard that Gus was there, they wanted to meet this important official that their parents know. This is an opportunity to talk to Gus, or Audee-El, which is the name he is known by. They want to expand their understanding of the kingdom as it grows and changes all around them.

Adam and John are like sponges, they ask questions and get answers that they can trust, they take it all in, and are having a great time. After a little while Adam asks Gus about the "release". The release of Satan at the end of the age, they know what the Bible say's but they want to get a law enforcement view of this coming event. [56]

95

Gus responds, "First of all, never let anyone tell you it is a myth, or that it is misinterpreted in the Bible, or that it had already happened during Armageddon. It will happen at the end of one thousand years from the day of the Lord., about eight hundred years from now.

Your parents, Sean and Laura, will not live that long, but you will, if you have no accidents. No Enoshe can live beyond one day, a day being one thousand years in the site of the Lord. The original Adam, the first man, was judged and told that he would die in the day of his sin. He nor any of his children have lived beyond one thousand years, although some, like Methuselah came close." [57]

Gus continues, "Satan's release will not be with a great fan fair, He will be very subtle and work behind the scenes to turn hearts from the Lord. He will question and deny everything you know about the Lord. He will question his origin, his motives, his honesty and his agenda."

Gus explains, "Satan will claim that Jesus is not God, but only the leader of several races of aliens, they live on another planet which is dying, and they came here to take our planet. Our twentieth century civilizations were very advanced and would have soon been able to resist the invasion. He will also assert that the world before the war was nearing a state of perfection, and that the world was at peace, till Jesus and his army of thugs swooped in to take over, and destroyed all the remnants of man's past."

Gus stops his answer, and turns to Sean, and asks, "Do they know? Do they know what they are called to do?"

Sean answers, "Yes, yes, they do, they know it all."

John chimes in, "We want to hear the information from someone else besides our father, we want to hear it confirmed to us. We believe it will help our resolve when the time comes."

Gus replies, "You two can trust your father to tell you the truth, he has no reason to lie, he is as honest as anyone I know. He knows what happened in the world before Jesus came to stop the evil of Satan, He will not exaggerate, he saw the nations being destroyed one after the other."

Gus continues, "You will also need to get the leader of the rebellion to go with you to Petra prior to the outbreak of the next war. He must be there with you when you discover the chamber with the equipment from before Armageddon. So, he cannot dispute the origin of the information and equipment. Once it is understood and documented by you and the others there at the discovery, it must be made public in the frontier communities all over the kingdom, you can use angels and saints to accomplish this portion. You can use ophanim for the discovery phase of your mission. You can only get into, and out of Petra from overhead. You must use a saint named Thomas Taylor to make your arrangements with the angels, he can be trusted, no one else. If you are successful in your mission and the nations hear and see the evidence, thousands will turn back to Jesus and run back to Jerusalem, for the protection of the Lord. Thousands of souls are in the balance."

Then Gus says, "Lets pray to the Lord for guidance." After praying, Adam and John go to bed in the bunk house, which is attached to the main house, and Gus, goes to a guest room in the main house, no one goes out in the dark to go home.

After some time of sleeping, a bright light enters Gus's bedroom, and he is awakened, the lights are from angels, and they begin to discuss some things with him. After a few moments Gus is whisked away by the angels, but not before most everyone in the house are awake and aware of the angels, in and around the house. But because they had been warned about the possible intrusion, everyone just rolled over and went back to sleep. Sean had even told the dogs, that there may be angels around the house tonight, and that they should not respond, they understood and agreed to be quiet. Sean also asked the dogs to go around the barn and animal pins to tell the other animals what Sean has said, again they agreed and began to alert the barn yard animals.

In the morning Gus came down stairs to the dinning room for breakfast. He saw Laura and several of her daughters working in the kitchen, and he apologized for the intrusion last night.

Laura says, "I didn't hear you come back; you must have been very discreet."

Before Gus could answer, Sean and about eight sons, came crashing in, they had just finished their early chores and were back to get their breakfast. Sean asked Gus to come and sit next to him.

Sean asked Gus, "So what happened in the middle of the night? Can you tell us?"

Gus responds, "I can tell you the basics but not the details, there was a band of rustlers taking cattle up between the farms. They hid the cattle in the daytime and then move them discreetly in the night. They steal cattle in the south and take them to the frontier in the north."

Sean asks, "Why do they need to steal cattle, is there a shortage?"

Gus adds, "No, these rustlers are stealing the cattle for the underground meat market, they will slaughter and eat them back at their homesteads."

Sean looks perplexed and asks, "Why? We don't need to eat meat."

Gus, "Well the best we can figure is that the pre-Armageddon culture of these people was meat eating, and very little crop raising. They know it is illegal but old habits die hard. The good news is that the animals are in good enough condition to testify against the rustlers. Some times the rustlers cut out the tongues of their victims. But these men used muzzles to keep them quiet.

Sean say's to Gus, "I'm going to miss having you around, when you come to our area promise me, you'll stop in, and bring your wife as well."

Gus say's "Will do."

CHAPTER NINE

Audee-El and David

It's been thirty-five years since Gus was at Sean's house, and Sean and Laura are on the roof top enjoying the evening when a messenger comes to the front door.

Inner city or rural mail delivery is mostly done by malaks, angels, this is because of their ability to cover large distances quickly.

The message is from Jerusalem, it says that, "Audee-El, aka Gus G. Hubbard, has died and is translated home, to his new home in the third heaven. A gathering of his family and friends will be made in seven days, in Jerusalem. The gathering is being held by the Lord Jesus Christ and will be at pavilion 6 in the outer temple court. Transportation will be provided for you and any of your family who knew Audee-El personally. Audee-El was a faithful servant and beloved of the Father."

The list of attendees came easily and a return message sent, there will be seven attending, from Sean's clan.

Some interesting changes had happened to Gus since his night spent at Sean's house. He had evidently enjoyed talking to Sean's sons and daughters so much, that he decided that he wanted to have some direct family from Vera in his old age. The Lord gave him a son, just one year after that night with Sean. Gus named him David, after the greatest Jewish king to ever live.

Since Vera's sons from her first husband had left home eighty years earlier, and went to live in the northern settlements, Gus was able to spend most of his free time with David. David is now thirty-three years old, and it is said that he looks so much like Gus that it's scary.

At the gathering there is an emphasis on the positive aspects of being translated to heaven, seeing the father, and having been changed from corruption to incorruption. Gus is now a saint. Sean and Laura are amazed at the sheer number of angels and saints in attendance. One after another complimented Gus for his character, his convictions and his compassion. They kept saying that he was a very special Enoshe, he could receive and act on orders almost instantly.

Gus also has literally hundreds of Enoshe law enforcement officers in attendance.

After the official activities were done, the complete news crew, the five others, Sean, Laura, Isaac, Sally, Evelyn and their families are gathered with Vera and her three sons. They are all enjoying refreshments and sharing stories about Gus.

One of Sean's sons mentions to Nicolas, Vera's oldest son, how proud he must be of Gus. Only to hear him mutter back that, "Gus was just one of Jesus's duped minions, he did what he was told and now he's dead…" He continued, "where we live, up north, we don't need your Jesus, we can get along just fine without him, we'll make our own laws thank you."

The members of the news team were surprised to hear the comment, because they had just finished having a very pleasant conversation with Vera's sons, even to the point of exchanging addresses and family names.

When Vera heard what Nicolas had said, she quipped in anger. "Nicolas! you two can leave now."

The two sons just stare at their mother momentarily and with pure anger in their eyes they turn and storm out. Vera turns to the news crew and say's, "I'm sorry that you had to hear that, you are all like family to me, and it hurts me that they are so angry with God. They were angry when they left to move north, Gus and I had hoped that they might soften with time, but it hasn't happened. I'm not at all sure why they even came today."

Vera continues, "I was hoping, when I heard they were coming that they wanted to meet their half brother David, but they would not come to the house before the service to meet him, and they came late to the service itself. They never said anything to David at all."

Sally says, "We have their addresses, we'll write to them and let them know that it was nice meeting them."

Vera says, "If you have their address please let me know what it is. I don't actually have it. They mail me without return addresses. I only know the community name."

Sally shows her the addresses, and Vera say's "This can't be correct, this is a location two hundred miles east of their community."

Isaac says, "They have given us false information, this was a one-way exchange, but why?"

Sean says, "Regardless of why, we all want to talk to David and get to know him."

As it turns out, everyone agrees that getting to know and talking to David is like talking to their old friend Gus, what a wonderful time they all had.

CHAPTER TEN

Droughts and Plagues

It is the second week of the seventeenth jubilee, which is slightly more that eight hundred years after the day of the Lord, when Jesus redeemed Jerusalem. The governing council of the Association of Northern Settlements, (ANS) is having an emergency meeting.

The association had sent a delegation of twelve men, from different northern areas to Jerusalem, to ask the Lord for his assistance in combating certain problems they are experiencing. Certain sections of the northern settlements are suffering a drought, and it has become serious, it is now about the sixth year for many of the communities. The other problem they are having is a sickness, there are two settlements on the far north frontier that have developed a contagious illness, the virus is actually killing some of the settlers. The delegation has just returned and is preparing to report their findings.

The chairman of the association calls the meeting to order and hands the podium over to the delegation. The leader of the delegation and his companions all set across the front of the room. They look like they are ready to die, they are as grim as they can be. They just stare straight forward and show no emotions at all.

The leader starts out by saying that they approached the Lord and informed him as to their mission, "We told him about our problems and that we would like his assistance in solving them, could he help us."

He continued, "The Lord asked us if we had not read, or do not remember what was written by Zachariah the prophet at the end of his prophecy?" I was silent, and the Lord continued, "Scripture made clear that the families of survivors of Armageddon are required to come to Jerusalem to celebrate the feast of tabernacles once ever year. If any of the nations do not come up, the punishment will be droughts and plagues." [58]

The leader asked the Lord, "Do you mean that the plagues and droughts are being caused by you?"

The Lord replies, "I have many laws, for almost everything that happens in earth and in heaven, and if any of them are ignored or deliberately violated there will be a punishment or judgment imposed. The requirement of the nations and Jerusalem is no exception.

Because you and the nations are Enoshe, and are incapable of keeping my laws, you fall short of my glory, I have provided a path of grace and mercy through my blood at the cross.

For eight hundred years I have provided a world with real peace and without war, famine, drought, earthquakes, storms, violence, a world with plenty of food and water., all of this with little or no requirements on your part. Yet, the requirement of attending a feast, a celebration, is too much for me to ask?

I will advise you the same way as I did for Adams first born son, Cain, when his sacrifice was not acceptable, 'if thou doest well, you will be accepted, if not, sin is laying at the door.'"

The Lord continued, "I desire to bless everyone, your choices will determine your future."

The leader of the delegation stops, and sits down. And asks, "Are there any questions?"

One of the council members shouts, "Is that it!! Did he offer to help? Is he going to send angels or more saints?"

Leader, "No, no direct aid will be coming. He has inferred that a proper response on our part will correct the problems and the plague will be stayed."

The entire council erupts into shouting and anger, Jesus is accused of spiritualizing the problems, when what is needed, are real world assistance, not religious mumbo jumbo, we need help now!

After a while the anger begins to decline and things calm down. A show of hands reveals that only six settlements of the dozens which make up the association, have been ignoring the Jerusalem requirements. When it is found that these settlements also represent the areas most affected by the droughts and plagues, they are persuaded to go straight way to Jerusalem to apologize to the Lord, they begrudgingly agree to comply.

The rest of the representatives agree to start raising taxes for the purpose of building dams and canals for the storage and movement of water from place to place. This is meant to reduce the settlements reliance on rain. They also agree to build infirmaries and start training health care people for any future outbreaks. There are no doctors at this time because for eight hundred years there was no diseases or ailments, only cuts and abrasions, even broken bones were rare.

As the representatives adjourn and begin to leave the meeting, two of the delegates slip quietly out of the building and begin the long trip home to the southern edge of the northern district. These men are Sean's sons, Adam and John they are the senior elders of their family. Sean, Laura and the other four members of the news crew are gone, they died hundreds of years ago, it's now up to their children to move the family forward. Adam and John are not travelling alone, they are too old. There are twelve younger grandsons there to provide protection and travelling assistance along the way.

The settlements in the south, closer to Jerusalem are much more devout to Jesus, and further north you can feel much more tension when it comes to spiritual and religious issues. Adam and John are not at all comfortable in the northern frontier, they know that they should keep their opinions to themselves, there is a very definite rift forming between the devout Christians and independent thinking settlers of the outlying frontier.

On the way home from the meeting, a trip which takes weeks, Adam and John discuss the need to search for the Petra equipment, which was left by their parents. They decide to contact the other families on the way home and consult them concerning the timing. And to begin to plan the operation.

Adam and John determine to first stop at Evelyn's family farms, they too are further south.

When they approach Evelyn's children, they are cordial and friendly, but they don't seem to quite know what Adam and John are talking about. They are asked to produce the journals so that they can be made to understand what is required. They remember the journals but haven't seen them in hundreds of years. Never the less an exhaustive search was made, but to no avail. Evelyn's family is genuinely upset that the book is lost, they can't believe that it is just lost. Adam, John and their entourage leave for Isaac and Sally's home, which is much closer to Sean's homestead.

When Adam and John discuss the book with Isaac's eldest living son, he's completely on board with their thoughts to begin the mission. The book and some other old artifacts are locked away in a small room off of Isaac's master bed room in the main house. Every one goes to the main house to get the book to make sure what it says, and to see what other artifacts are there.

Everyone is shocked when they are told that not only is the book missing, but everything in the room is gone, stripped bare. This can't be! Was the cry, when they saw the room.

Isaac's sons convened a family meeting of everyone that has had access to the room in the past five hundred years, and inquiry is made, it took two days to complete, but it was concluded that some one had stolen the book hundreds of years earlier. The family is devastated and angry, they are intent that they will find the thief.

Adam and John console them as much as they could, but they are told that they must not tell anyone, outside their family that the book is missing, they should act as though nothing has happened.

The trip home for Adam and John continues, and is soon complete. Between the horrible spiritual condition of the northern brethren, and the loss of the journal books of the other families, it was a truly depressing trip. They retire for the night and agree to get their family books in the morning when they are rested.

The next day after breakfast the two men went into the old bedroom of Sean and Laura, the books are kept in a chest at the foot of their bed. The room has not been used since they died, so long ago. The room is now a guest room. And only occasionally used, but the chest remains. They began systematically removing the locks, then, they could tell that the hasp was not attached to the chest at all, it had been chiseled lose and tucked behind the hanging locks.

Everyone knew immediately what the broken hasp means, and no one wants to look in the chest, but they did, and sure enough the books are gone. All the five books, written by the news reporters have been stolen.

Adam and John begin to plan a way forward, they wonder if they can remember enough about the facts to reproduce the directions in the books and find the equipment in Petra. They begin right away and also sent messages to the other families to solicit information and memories from them to fill in the gaps.

It has taken several weeks to assemble everything together, but it's clear that even if they can find the equipment, they would have no idea how to operate any of it.

John has an idea that Gus's son, David should be asked if he has any information from his father, a messenger was sent to Jerusalem to inquire.

The next morning an ophan arrives at Sean's home, David is carried within the ophan and is delivered to the house. He is greeted and taken inside. Adam, John and David sit down and discuss the missing books.

David asks, "Are all the books the same or are there differences?"

John replies, "No they are all direct copies of each other, each book has all five journals and the directions to the site."

David opens the case that he is carrying, and says, "This is the book that my father gave me for safe keeping, won't it work? My father told me that he did not trust his step sons with the book, or the knowledge of the book, I was to never tell them anything."

John replies, "Gus had a book? of course, each member received a copy, Gus did not write a journal, but he was still a member of the team. David, may I see the book?"

John systematically looks through the pages, and stops, then he says, "Yes it will! Praise God! The mission is on. David would you like to be a part?"

David responds, "Yes I would, I would like to honor my father, he has also given me some good connections."

John replies in a serious tone, "David, who else knows you are here, and why you have come? We have enemies which would still steal this book if they can, if they are from the northern settlements, they are also capable of violence. We must be very discrete with all our communications. Your brothers must not get wind of any of your information. You must have a good cover story for your time spent with us. David, souls are at risk."

David replies, "Roger that."

CHAPTER ELEVEN

Azazel
The Peoples Man

It is now only months from the end of the millennium, the one-thousand-year time of peace and the reign of Jesus in Jerusalem. Nearly everyone on earth knows that the Bible, in the book of Revelations teaches that Satan will be released from sheol, the pit, and allowed to go about the earth deceiving the peoples. [59]

No one knows just how this will happen, or what he will look like. Some people think he will show himself as the great red dragon of Revelations chapter twelve, others think he will look like Pan, the horned pagan god, which is half man and half goat, still others think he will appear as Bel, the angel of light, the bright one with his great wings.

Some people believe he will have an entourage of mighty angels and demons, and will be prepared to face down Jesus. Regardless of who you hear, in the frontiers they believe it will be a spectacular revealing event, that no one will forget or miss.

For the past five years there is a middle-aged man, (which means he's over one-hundred years old) named Azazel, living in the deep north settlements, he is a musician and singer, he has been a critic and opponent of God's kingdom and Jesus specifically. His music and lyrics reflect his hatred of the things of God. However, he has managed to stay just outside any direct action against him by law enforcement, but he is continually pushing his position. Azazel is a solo performer;

he plays a guitar tells satiric jokes and sings; he travels alone from settlement to settlement in a large circuit.

When the day came that the thousand years were expired, the devout Enoshe believers in Jesus are having large prayer meetings to prepare for the event. The backslidden Enoshe are throwing parties to greet, whatever the day brings.

The news crew's children have been planning a mission to go to Petra with the hopes of persuading some of the members of the northern leadership, to show them how truthful Jesus has been about the past ages. Sean's and Gus's children are prepared to move as soon as they see how Satan will go public. The anticipation world-wide is incredibly high and palpable.

As it happens, Satan is a no show, after three days of waiting and praying nearly all the prayer meetings, disband and go to their homes. The rebellious frontier Enoshe even begin to drift back to their homes.

While Satan made no appearance in public, he was released from his cell. He was taken from his cell, and escorted by a band of God's angels to a location outside Jerusalem.

He was shown boundaries around Jerusalem and Israel the land, where he can not operate, if he is found within Israel or Jerusalem, he will be taken directly back to his cell, but not before he is publicly displayed and humiliated. He is also told that he is to limit his operations, deceptions and temptations to the gentile nations outside Israel.

Satan is taken to an undisclosed rural location and released, he looked at the angels for just a moment, then like a fish being released back into a lake, turned and disappeared into the night.

Three days later Azazel was finishing one of his concerts and the people were leaving, when an older man walked up to him and told him that he had been walking outside the settlement when he saw a flier nailed on a post, it announced that Azazel was playing tonight, and it explained that Azazel is a leading opponent of the government in Jerusalem. The old man asked, "Why haven't I heard of you before? You have a great show, your singing is good, your satire is spot on, and you have a good edge to your wit."

Azazel replies, "I'm a bit of a loner, and even my brother who is my only relative has disowned me years ago. I like performing, but beyond that I don't like people very much, The people like my jokes and songs a lot, but me, not so much. So, I travel alone, almost always walking between towns, sometimes it's weeks between appearances."

The old man replies, "So you're a gypsy," and laughed.

Azazel looks at the old man in a strange way, and asks, "What's a gypsy?"

The old man just says, "Never mind" and excuses himself, turns and walks away.

Azazel packs up his few belongings and goes to the outskirts of the settlement, where he has his camp. The camp is tucked back into the woods off the side of the road. After he was there for about an hour, and had a good camp fire burning, he looked up to see the old man from the concert, walking up to the camp from the road.

The old man asks if he can set down? And Azazel, surprised, reluctantly allowed the old man to sit down, but quickly tells him that he thought that he had made it clear that he is a loner and likes his privacy.

The old man apologizes and begins explaining that he has an offer to make. He wants to be Azazel's manager; he would be the man behind Azazel's message and his fans, the public. He feels that Azazel can be much more effective with his help. He even suggests that there should be organized groups that have the same basic beliefs that Azazel has. The old man feels that Azazel can be the foundation of a great movement.

Azazel does not seem very interested, but agreed to allow the old man to explain things in more detail, and to ask Azazel questions about himself, family, his contacts in each town and his personal likes and dislikes. This takes hours to go through, and afterward the old man gets up and says he'll come back tomorrow and they can talk again, then he walks away, disappearing down the road towards town.

The next morning the old man shows up with some breakfast from the inn in the town. He also has a day pack for walking with Azazel to the next settlement. They start talking right away and they don't stop until they stop for the night. It was a little strange when they stopped for lunch, the old man started playing Azazel's guitar and was playing in the same exact style as Azazel, he even could sing with the same flare. Azazel was amazed, he asked when did you learn to play like me? The old man just said that he'd been playing and singing for a long, long time.

After they make a camp, they continue to talk about Azazel's life and friends, Azazel asks the old man why he needs to know so much about his life? The old man said that he has to be able to respond to anyone's questions without having to guess.

That night Azazel performs a really good program and has people laughing at his jokes and satire, however at the end of the show he just closed in the same old manner and dismissed the people. Azazel looked around to see what if anything, the old man might say, but he wasn't there, Azazel thought that it was strange that he had left.

Azazel goes to the camp after the show, and is surprised to find the old man there. He has the fire already burning and some hot drinks steeping in a pot. After they sit down to relax, the old man asks Azazel how he got his name, and does he know what it means?

Azazel replies, "My father gave me the name, he told me it means to wander or roam about. I think that's why I wander from place to place singing."

The old man say's, "That's pretty close to what it means, I know the person who was the first to have that name."

Azazel looks at the old man with a questioning look, "How do you know he is the first, how can you be sure?"

The old man replies, "Because, I've known him for seven thousand years, in fact until just a few days ago he was in prison with me, although not in the same cell."

Azazel indignantly retorts, "That's stupid, no one lives for seven thousand years, what is your name? tell me what is your name!"

The man replies, "I have many names, and they all fit me to a tee, Heylel, or Lucifer, Bel, the bright one, Pan the horned half man and half goat, or Apollyon lord of the pit, and your favorite, Satan, the adversary, oh, and don't forget the Devil."

Azazel snaps back, "Shut up, that's not funny, Satan is supposed to be an angel, and your no angel!"

Then in a flash of light the old man is transformed as the angel Heylel, right in front of Azazel, and then a voice is heard from the woods, shouting, "Run, Run, Run away,"

Before Azazel could make a move Heylel touches him on his shoulder, and he is paralyzed in place. Heylel instantly disappears as he flies upward, he begins to fly around the area to find the person who shouted a warning to Azazel. But there is no one in the area, there is only a small group of horses grazing in the pasture behind the trees.

Perplexed, but confident that there is no one in the area, he returns to the camp, and takes up his position next to the paralyzed Azazel, whose eyes, are full of terror, He begins explaining to Azazel, that he is perfect for his needs, I have no servants, no resources no assets at all, I have to steal everything that I need.

You have a reputation of opposition to Jesus and have been travelling around, stirring things up. I'm going to steal your identity, I was going to just use you and work behind you, but you're a loser, you have no vision no energy, no real direction or goals. You will just dwindle away in self destruction, I'm just going to speed that up, your life will be valuable to my new movement.

Heylel touches Azazel on the shoulder, to release him, and then with one swing delivers a death blow. Azazel slumps over and is gone in a moment. Heylel quickly relieves him of all his personal affects and clothes, and takes the body away to destroy it. Just before dawn Heylel comes back to the camp, wearing the freshly laundered clothes of Azazel and looking just like him, Heylel's copy, or impersonation of Azazel is amazing he is completely the same, even the little traits and habits.

As the sun begins to come up two Enoshe law enforcement officers come walking up to the camp. They introduce themselves to the new Azazel, as he is cooking some food on the camp fire, he offers a hot drink to the officers, they respectfully decline. The officers ask him if he is okay?

Azazel replies, "Yes I am, why do you ask?"

They reply, "We have received a report that you had been killed last night by another man that was with you."

Azazel laughs and says, "I think someone is pulling your chain, who told you that?

The officer says, "A little bird told us,"

Azazel continues, "The old man that was here last night left before I went to bed, he probably went straight back to the settlement, he had stopped because he likes guitar music."

The officers continue to ask Azazel questions about himself, to establish his identity, after a while, they are satisfied that he is Azazel the singer, and they walk away. As they begin to leave Azazel picks up his guitar and begins to practice for the next show, which is that night.

The show that night was a great success, in fact some of the people who have heard Azazel before, thought that he had improved his guitar playing and was a little more animated than they remembered. They figured he had been practicing, and maybe he is invigorated by the Satanic no show. Azazel had long maintained that there is no Satan, that Satan is just a myth to cause fear in the weak minded. He blamed Jesus and the saints for perpetuating the lie.

The main difference between this show and the one last night, is the that Azazel, (the new Azazel) asked if anyone wanted to stay around after the show to talk and begin to network with each other, he would stay as well. He was amazed by the large number of the audience who stayed behind.

Azazel's movement has started, a movement to discredit Jesus and his kingdom.

It's been nearly two years since Azazel's movement started at the concert. His call to rebellion has struck a chord with the frontier settlers who want to live without any obligation to Jerusalem, Jesus or his rod of iron.

Azazel has his view of the world which he presents to the people, it tells them what they want to hear. First of all, he acknowledges that Jesus is a very powerful and great being, but denies that Jesus is the Son of God.

He asserts that Jesus is the leader of a race of aliens which came to the earth to disinherit the Enoshe and they live here while their home planet is being regenerated. The saints of Jesus are here to rule this world with him till they no longer need the Enoshe.

Azazel, claims that the angels of God are also races from the other planet, they are also working with Jesus to add control over the people. He says that the angels are not very smart and are duped by Jesus and used as thugs to spy on the people. He maintains that regardless of what people have been told, there aren't really millions of angels, only a few thousand.

He claims that the world that existed before Jesus came to earth, was actually a very progressive and beautiful world, which had been at peace for years and was solving all the worlds health issues through their technology and ingenuity. Humans had been travelling to the moon and flying around the world faster than the speed of sound.

This wonderful world that Azazel presented had the ultimate in personal freedom, everyone was able to live is own life, without government interference or high taxes, and of course no tithing to God.

There was no tithing because they believed that God did not create the world, it was a natural process. So, God has no right to impose his values on the Enoshe.

He also asserts that if the world before Jesus, had seen the problem coming, they could have united, resisted and defeated the aliens.

When people question Azazel, as to where he got his information, how do you know these things? He simply refers to an angelic source which has turned against Jesus, and that he has confirmed it from several other angels which are discontented. Azazel has at times, when in private, asserted that there would be a host of angels that might fight with the Enoshe should they rebel against Jesus.

Azazel's movement is growing like wild fire, he has representatives going out in all directions telling everyone what his message is. The movement is growing in the four corners of the kingdom, it's working from the outside and moving in. The truly devout Christian Enoshe live closer to Israel and Jerusalem.

CHAPTER TWELVE

Petra the Mission

Two hundred years have passed After finding his father's copy of the book of journals, made by the news crew, David Ben Audee-El the son of Gus Hubbard has become an Enoshe law enforcement officer, just like his father. He has moved up in the Lord's service and is a devout Christian.

David's half-brothers from his mother side, have on several occasions attempted to learn the status of any attempts to recover the equipment in Petra. David's mother has been interrogated by her sons, no one is sure how they learned about the equipment, but it must have been a slip by Vera or Gus at some time in the past.

The idea that they are still asking about the equipment and any possible attempt to recover it, means that whoever stole the books is still looking to stop any recovery. It has been a topic of prayer that Vera will not give into her sons, and give them the information. Evidently the brothers do not know that there is a sixth book.

Shortly after bringing the sixth book to Sean's grandson, John, a meeting was held at a secret location to plan an expedition to Petra for the recovery. The meeting included Thomas Taylor, the saint that was at Petra at the time of the evacuation, his contribution will be valuable to their success. They decided that their first action will be a trip, to see what the situation at Petra's entrance is like, and see if it is guarded.

John has a group of six of his great, great grandsons to come with the expedition when the recovery is attempted. David saw

John's sons come into the room and stood up to greet them, he smiled and commented, "These men are not only devout, but they are also stout, I'm glad they are on my side."

One of the problems with the expedition is transportation, While Thomas Taylor can disappear and just show up in another location and no one knows how he got there or where else he went while he was gone, John and his men must travel by foot or horseback. David has connections for using Ophans, this is because of his law enforcement requirements.

It is decided that John and his men will travel in Ophans as directed by David, and stagger their travel times to make it hard to associate their travel with each other. Their travel will appear to be part of law enforcement activities.

A location just outside the old entrance to Petra is chosen for the group to rendezvous, they can all wait to appear at that coordinate until when there is no one around, because the Ophan can cloak they're appearance, this includes they're passengers. As it is, there is no one around, the area is a beautiful green location. There are fields of fruit and olive trees. After 1000 years of rain fall and love and care from the farmers the land is blooming like a rose.

The rock face where the entrance was is completely backfilled and overgrown. It was instantly obvious that there is no way into Petra thru the old canyon. They begin to consider other ways to get in to the fortress. They decided to go over the cliffs and go down inside, and look for a way out from the inside. They all load into the Ophan and travel to the backside of the cliffs, when they come down, they can hardly tell where they are. They're first task is to find the old Siq entrance. It takes hours but they finally find the location they think is it, only remnants of it still exist. Part of the problem within Petra is that there is now some water in the bottom of the basin. This makes some of the landmarks indicated in the journals, difficult or impossible to find.

One of John's grandsons asks the question, "How is the water getting out of the basin, where is it going?" The group all start following the flow of the water, they finally walk around a large boulder in the bottom of the basin and there it is, the old Nabatean drain tunnel that was hewn through the rock wall. It was made in ancient times to provide a secondary path for flood waters, and it is still there, partially filled with some fallen rock and washed-in sand.

The group takes a little time to look at the area within Petra which is believed to have the equipment tunnel location. They are somewhat encouraged because the area is not underwater or disturbed, like much of the other areas. Before leaving the Petra area they search for the external exit of the emergency water tunnel outside Petra, they find it slightly north-east of the original entrance, it is hidden back against the rock wall, covered by brush and trees, it appears as a very small spring flowing from the rocks. It doesn't look like anyone is aware of the tunnel or using the immediate area.

They all agree on another trip to the site with the tools to attempt to open the drainage tunnel should happen as soon as everyone can schedule it.

The team agrees that the northern leadership people who should be on hand when the equipment is recovered, must be able to come into Petra and remove the equipment without any help from saints or Ophans. They would not believe that the equipment and data was real if they don't find it themselves. This is risky because there are no guarantees that the equipment can be found or is still operable, after all it's been over a thousand years.

It's been three months since the first trip to Petra, the expedition team is assembled just north of Jerusalem and they load into an Ophan for the trip south to Petra. This time they go directly to the inside of Petra at the emergency flood tunnel. They are all carrying hand tools to clear the tunnel, shovels, picks and hoes. They begin to remove all the sand first, then they work on breaking the larger rocks which are fallen from the ceiling, and carry them out.

The expedition had arrived in Petra early in the morning and worked all day, they estimate that they are about eighty percent through the tunnel when they finally stop for the day, they go to look around the area where the hidden equipment chamber may be. They are shocked to find that someone else has been digging into the rock entrances of many of the old tombs. It does not appear that anything had been found or removed. The recollection of Thomas Taylor, is that everything in the hide-a-ways which were used by the one hundred and forty-four thousand Jews were destroyed as part of God's cleansing. But the tunnel of the news crew is in a location deeper into Petra, because the crew came so late in the last three and one-half years. He doesn't remember the equipment being destroyed, and he feels there is a chance that it's still there. He's not sure that anything will still operate, even if it is found, one thousand years is a long time.

The expedition sets up camp for the night at a location near the flood tunnel, they begin to speculate as to who has been in Petra? Whoever it is, they somehow managed to find a way in, but how?

The next day the crew manages to finish their digging out, of the water tunnel and to allow it to drain more completely than it has been, they are careful not to cause any interest from outside the tunnel by making a mess. They can now enter and exit Petra on foot and also carry equipment in and out. They stash the tools inside Petra and reluctantly go home. The mission will now become more political, they must convince a group of northern leadership to go to Petra with them, this could take time.

John, as a senior elder of the clan Wright, has many contacts with the leaders of the other clans, tribes. He has a feel, from the many conferences and committees, who shares his views and those who don't. He must approach those who don't believe that Jesus has been truthful about his origins and nature, and see if they are so intrenched in their position that they cannot be swayed by the truth.

No one in the expedition has seen any of the Petra evidence, they are accepting their parent's testimony as true, only Thomas Taylor actually knows what to expect, and he as a saint, is considered by the northern leaders to be the enemy, and not at all trust worthy.

It has become obvious that the settlements and tribes from all over the world have become so tainted concerning Jesus and his government, that a civil war seems to be the only possible outcome, it's only a matter of time. Insurrection is being pushed by people like Azazel, who are preaching hatred.

John has contacted a number of officials and leaders of the clans, he has managed to set up a meeting at a neutral location just north of the Wright estates, John's home. This meeting is the eighth time that the meeting has been scheduled and subsequentially changed, emergencies seem to keep coming up to stop the meeting, it's clear that the project has opposition, but John, who is now nearly one thousand years old, and his grand sons are determined to make it happen.

John and his grandson set out on horse back and carriages to go to the meeting, it is still a two-day journey. While they are yet twenty miles out from the location, they are travelling down the road and find a roadblock. The men at the roadblock inform John that there is plague in the area and that they cannot go any further, you must turn around now.

John explains that they must pass, and that it is important that they make it to the meeting. The men at the roadblock become angry and begin to force John's group backward. John explains that this group is immune to the plague and that they must pass. The men are now shouting antichristian slurs and cursing at Johns group. The grandsons won't take this without a fight. They remount their horses and pull out their pikes. Just as it seems that violence will ensue, a group of Enoshe law enforcement officers emerge from the forest on each side of the road, there are also two Ophans now hovering overhead. The conflict is over before it began, the men at the roadblock are arrested and the roadblock destroyed, not just taken apart, dissolved.

David steps out of one of the Ophans and greets John, he assures him that there is no plague in this area, and there are no other roadblocks between them and their destination.

John, looking very relieved smiled at David and said, "I should have known you would have our backs."

They proceed to the meeting, and there are eight northern clans represented, while the meeting was reasonably civil, the tension was heavy and the leaders showed no trust in the expedition, they generally felt that it was a trap to expose them to the Jerusalem government by having them travel through Israel and Jerusalem, without going to the temple.

John kept going back to the threat and realities of war, do you really want to see your families decimated, do you really want to make killers out of your children? Is it not worth a try, to stop the war? A war which may be based on lies, if Jesus is who he says, then you're in grave danger.

In the end, three of the eight leaders agreed to join the expedition, each leader will have two body guards, for a total of nine additional members. The grand sons of John can go early by Ophan with David, but everyone else must ride in wagons or on horseback. The expedition will be scheduled for seven days at the site, with the possibility of more time if agreed upon by everyone.

There is one caveat that came out of the meeting, the leaders only agreed to go if Azazel the singer could come with them. They felt that because he is so central to the opposition movement that if he was not included, no one would believe the outcome. Azazel has his own travel network and would come and go by his own means, so he is not included in the travel plans.

John reluctantly agreed, so long as the expedition could start immediately without delay. Everyone agreed and coordinates were supplied for Azazel to rendezvous with them at Petra.

The expedition starts at a location just slightly north of where the old Syrian city of Aleppo would be, if it still existed. They travel almost directly south, which brings them just east of the Lebanon mountain range, and west of the old location of Damascus.

They stay on the high country to the east of Jerusalem and the dead sea, this path would have been nearly impassable except since the rains have come all over the area, it has been revived and cultivated, there are now roads going all along the ridge, and descending down into the Petra area. This path was chosen to keep them as far from Jerusalem as possible, without completely circling around. It has taken nearly a week to get to Petra and the coordinates that they gave to Azazel. They actually arrive late in the evening and decide to go inside in the morning, besides Azazel has not yet shown up.

The men agree to go on into the stronghold and begin searching, they will leave several men behind outside the tunnel to wait for Azazel, then to guard the entrance from any interference outside. The water tunnel is quite large in diameter and can accommodate horses with packs.

Once inside the stronghold the expedition recovers the digging tools left behind by the previous visit. They proceed along the north edge of the basin, for about two miles, skirting the water in the bottom, the water level has dropped by several feet since the flood tunnel was cleaned out, the tunnel itself is now dry, only wet moist sand in the bottom. Once they reach the original canyon entrance, they start backtracking the directions given by the news team in their journals.

It might seem that retracing the news crews track would be a simple task, the news crew were detail-oriented people, professionals. They were continually asking questions and making observations of everything around them, especially Sally, who was a photographer, she analyzes everything she saw and determined if it was important or would make a great photo, she would even wait in one place for the light to change, to make the photo better.

Sally's details have been to a large extent washed away, by a thousand years of erosion from wind and water. However, she often would describe a setting by the large rock features all around it, she would describe the folds in the rocks and layering of the cliffs. These larger features have not been destroyed by time, even though they are sand stone, they are still there.

The expedition decided to wait for awhile to see if Azazel shows, and to allow him some time to catch up to them, Back at the entrance Azazel just walked up from nowhere, the horses were startled as he passed between two of them, one horse literally jumped back ten feet to the side and looked at Azazel, who turned and looked back at the horse. When he saw the horse staring at him, he said, "What are you looking at?"

The horse said, "I don't know".

There were also some birds in the bushes nearby, one of the birds said, "I don't know either but it's not human!"

Before Azazel could do anything, the horse turned and ran into the field yelling, "Run, run!"

The entrance guards came running and asked Azazel what just happened? And, Azazel said, "That horse can talk!" The guards just say, "Yes of course, all animals can talk." Then they ask him to come with them, the others are waiting for you inside Petra.

As they lead Azazel into Petra, he is perplexed by what had just happened. Animals could not talk when he was placed in prison, he is trying to remember why the horses voice seems familiar?

They soon come to the expedition near the old entrance, and join the others, they begin moving north-east towards the area indicated by the News crew. Azazel determines that he is going to be as disruptive as possible, he is constantly making snide comments about Johns grandsons and how dishonest the news crew has been about the past. He makes fun of the whole expedition, how it is a waste of time, and if they can't find the equipment right away that he's leaving.

The representatives from the northern settlements are embarrassed by the conduct of Azazel, and they try to get him to back-off, they even take him aside to talk with him, but to no avail. At one-point Azazel points to something on the rocks and insists that the expedition turn aside and investigate the area, and of course there is nothing there.

Johns grandsons, know how important the expedition is, and are determined to endure any and all insults to see it through. David is with the expedition, but not wearing any uniform or indicating in any way that he is an Enoshe law enforcement officer, he has spent hundreds of years studying every detail written in the Journals and every drawing and diagram made by all the members of the crew. He feels like he could go through the site blind folded., he is confident that he can find the location.

After hours of searching the group stops for a lunch break, David asks if he could go on his own and continue searching, he is given leave, but told not to go too far without checking in.

After about thirty minutes David comes back and asks for some lunch, all of the younger men tease him about not being able to skip lunch. After eating for a little while, David takes John to the side and tells him that he had found the site, and would show them all after lunch. John can only look at David and marvel, because he was able to control his emotions.

John asks, "Are you sure?"

David responds, "Yes, but there will be a lot of digging, mostly soft sand washed down from above. If we work hard, we'll be in today."

The expedition packs up and continues, they are told to follow David, of course, Azazel refuses to comply and is wandering about on his own, although not too far away. After about twenty minutes, David stops and asks the representatives to come to him and he removes a drawing made by Sally from his vest pocket, unfolds it and holds it up in front of everyone, and points to the rock formation in front of them. The rocks are exactly the same as the drawing. Sally had shown the entrance on the drawing, and that it was approximately one hundred feet from where she was making the drawing, she had even drawn an arrow to point out the location.

The representatives all got excited, and called for Azazel to come see. He reluctantly came to look, he was obviously angry, and simply said, "I'll believe it when I see it."

Six of the young men began to organize to dig the colluvial wash (sand and stones) away from the entrance. While they were working, the rest of the expedition went about building a camp site for that night.

David calls three of the body guards for the representatives over to him, to talk to them discreetly, he tells them that there was an incident at the entrance of Petra with the horses, and that the horses swear that there is something wrong with Azazel, "We don't know what it is, but don't let him get close to your representatives, we don't know what it means, but you can't be too careful." Then David says, "my father is Gus Hubbard, one of the news crew, that's why I'm here."

One of the guards responds, "Audee-El was your father? He was "ELE" wasn't he?"

"ELE" stands for "Enoshe Law Enforcement".

David replies, "Yes he was, and so am I."

The guards just say, "Thank you for the tip."

David was right, when he said that there is a lot of digging needed to open the enclosure. The diggers first have to shovel it up and throw it back out of the hole, and then someone else has to shovel the dirt to the left or right, this opens the area up and will allow direct access into the enclosure.

The diggers have been working for two hours non-stop and are now going to be spelled by others in the expedition. The first shift of diggers had moved nearly five yards of material from in front of the wall. The second shift had been digging for about an hour when one of them shouted, "There's a doorway!" As they continue digging it becomes clear that the opening in the rock is about six feet high and five feet wide. This is precisely the size given by the journals.

Everyone, except Azazel, is excited to think that they are about to open the enclosure, it's like looking into an Egyptian tomb and wondering if the mummy is still inside. The diggers get to a point that they can begin to look inside, they reflect a light back into the chamber and one of the diggers calls back, he says, "There is nothing in there, I don't see anything."

No sooner than he said that there is nothing there, Azazel shouts out, "You fool, you are all duped fools, what a waste of time!"

Then John shouts, "Wait a minute," and he leans over to the man looking into the chamber and tells him to crawl in for about eight feet and then look to the left. The man did what he was told and crawled in, Then, he called back out, "It's here, there's a lot of stuff in here."

They brought the man out and resumed digging the chamber out so they can remove the equipment. The next two hours was spent removing the equipment and inventorying the contents, everyone is amazed how many cases there were. Each case is a road case, which means it is weatherproof and completely sealed. The equipment inside is too valuable to get damaged by travel.

As the contents are being compared to the inventory provided by the news crew. They find that each item they find is within their own manufacturers case and then placed inside the equipment carrying case, and then placed with other equipment in the sealed road cases. As a result, the contents look absolutely perfect, like they were used yesterday, not even dusty. They had also packed all the manufacturers operating manuals, and trouble-shooting documents along with the equipment. Even the batteries were removed from the equipment and stored separately, they too are not damaged. The solar and manual battery chargers have been located as well.

The inventory and recovery, from the chamber, exceeds everyone's expectation, the excitement is amazing. They can't wait to get into the laptop computers to see the files.

Azazel, is standing a way off, watching what is happening, realizing that he can't allow this information to get out, He has come to the conclusion that he must stop the representatives from ever leaving Petra. He figures, he can make a cover story of how they were killed by others in the expedition, when the chamber was found empty. He will kill the leaders and disappear as quickly as possible, and make his way north. He knows that the guards will try to stop him, so he will need to become himself, and catch them off guard, or startle them by transforming himself.

The representatives are very impressed by the equipment and beginning to get into the excitement of the event. Azazel begins to walk up to them as though he would talk to them, but before he could get close, the guards stepped in front of him and ask him to step back, Azazel was angered and he triggered his response by transforming right in front of them. But they didn't even flinch, they instead took defensive actions and told the representatives to hit the deck which they did. Hay-lel, (Lucifer or Asshur) managed to hit one of the guards with a hard blow but the other guards step up and began to beat Hay-lel with their weapons and swords, they were like a pack of dogs, fearless, and too many for Hay-lel to defeat, he pulled his wings in and disappeared into the sky.

David ran to the bushes near the waters edge and called to some birds, gave them directions and sent them away, the birds flew away towards the entrance to Petra like they were shot out of a canon.

David had sent them to the entrance guards, to warn them that Lucifer was in the area and he may try to harm them, also the birds are to contact ELE and give them the code word "Witness", they will know what to do.

David approaches the representatives and tells them that he has sent for help from ELE and that if they wish, they can all be evacuated to a safe location in Jerusalem, where they can review, and analyze all the equipment and data from the site.

The representatives reluctantly agree, they realized that it was David's warning to the body guards that probably saved their lives. They also want the injured guard to get treatment.

Within five minutes there is a small fleet of Ophanim hovering overhead and picking up people and equipment as fast as they can, no one and nothing is left behind. They are all taken to a secure location within Jerusalem. Everyone in the expedition is in isolation at this secret place, they will remain there until the data can be assessed and a direction forward determined.

CHAPTER THIRTEEN

The Presentation

All the members of the Petra expedition have been brought back to Jerusalem, to a safe location. No one knows where, they are being kept hidden, this is for security reasons. The Petra equipment and artifacts are at the same location.

The expedition members themselves, know where they are, and are good with the location. They are in a secluded section of the Yahweh University. The saints which work at the university are attending their needs.

The representatives have asked to talk to ELE about the safety of their immediate families. They are very upset about the attack that Heylel made against them, and now they are concerned that their families are in danger from him. The entire clan is related to the representatives, how do you determine who is at the greatest risk?

The representatives have been informed that there is an exclusion zone in Israel in which Heylel is not allowed to enter or operate. If the people and animals, that are in danger go into this area, they will be safe. They must bring as much of their own provisions as possible. ELE will provide as much protection as they can, but there could be as many as twenty thousand people, from each tribe.

The leaders don't have a good feel for how many people of their tribes will want to relocate and leave their homes, and fields behind. They may wish to defend themselves. Three of the four tribes which were represented in Petra were leaning towards revolting from the kingdom, but when they saw the equipment, they now are embarrassed, because they had been so easily led away. They feel that Jesus is justified if he punishes them.

The leaders know what the Bible says about the final battle, or rebellion, that tribes of the world will come to the camp of the saints in Israel to take the kingdom from Jesus, but that fire will come down from heaven, and destroy them, and the earth. [59] Before the expedition these leaders did not fear the threat from the Bible, they were considered fables, to be laughed at, but not now, now they realize their dilemma.

The representatives are told that they need to assign their body guards to work out the details with ELE and their clan leaders, because the representatives themselves are required to be present, when the data and equipment from Petra is analyzed. They must see it all as it is revealed, so they can verify its validity.

The tedious process of going through everything in the data storage of the News crew, has begun. The representatives are stunned to see the true extent of the conditions in the world before and during the final days, it has been determined that a presentation of data and the old world will be made, for immediate release to the outskirts of the settlements, so they can compare what has been asserted by Azazel and others about the old world and Jesus's part in its destruction and the actual realities found in Petra.

First of all, the world was not an ideal world, there were hundreds of wars in the last hundred years, and dozens of wars in progress when the end came. There were famines all around the world, many nations were in chronic famine for years and years, in the last one hundred years leading up to the end, over fifty million people starved to death in Azazel's perfect world, and another one hundred and sixty million were killed in wars.

And these counts don't include the battles of Bet Sharrukin which killed over 600 million.

The high-tech civilization described by Azazel was only in some areas and the high-tech people had to a large extent denied the existence of God and the spirit realm, and they felt that life on earth had come from asteroids and comets from somewhere in the cosmos. The result of this is that they were only subject to their own personal values this caused widespread civil anarchy in the cities around the world, no one felt safe. They could take a baby from a mother's womb without any regret so long as they felt it was justified.

It became clear that if Jesus had not returned when he did, Bet Sharrukin would have destroyed nearly everyone on earth and Satan would have finished the job, Satan's goal was to destroy the seed of the woman.

The data from Petra included news file footage and stories about all aspects of society before the war, there are literally terabytes of data on stand-alone data storage books. You can simply enter a search parameter and the data would be presented with written articles and video support and interviews with relevant experts on the subjects. Political, religious, sports and social subjects could be explored with the lap top computers which each of the six members of the news crew had been using up until they left Petra. Several members had more than one computer for use with different purposes, some for their jobs and some for their personal use.

Evelyn was the communications expert for the news team, she had built a short-wave radio system for their use in Australia, it had been used for direct communication with the ships at sea and other radio operators around the world. There was also a global communications system that used short wave radio frequencies and dozens of small satellites in orbit around the world. The satellites received radio signals in Morse code and rebroadcast them back down to the surface of the earth.

The satellites are only the size of a loaf of bread, they could also transmit digital photos to and from radios. This system was still operating until the very end of the war, the network was called "CubeSat" and had been put in place for educational purposes, but while the internet communications could be interrupted, this system could continue to operate. There are photos from inside America after the nuclear attack, showing the devastation firsthand.

Yahweh university has the capability to produce visual presentations for their educational use. They can adapt the audio and videos computer files into their visual presentation formats. These presentations make an Imax film look primitive. They literally are suspended in open air, outside. They move and interact in real-time in 3D. The screen size for the presentation is a thousand feet long, and had has terrific sound projection.

Each of the clan representatives began producing presentations for the purpose of informing the Enoshe and Animals of the world, about their findings from Petra and give them the truth concerning Jesus and the coming war.

The presentations will include visual sites and sounds of life before the war. All of the clips will be selected by the Enoshe representatives of the clans, no suggestions or directions are from Jesus, or the saints that are helping them. Jesus has taken the position that the issue of the Enoshe rebellion is an Enoshe question and that he, Jesus will not interfere in their decisions, He feels they know the Gospel and they know what will happen to the rebellious, They, have to choose, each person for themselves. Whether to remove from the rebellion and take shelter in Israel, which he calls the "camp" or to fight against my kingdom. He simply says, "Come out of her my people."

The presentation includes clips of Hitler, and other world dictators, with their atrocities and world views. They also showing all sorts of lude behaviors and pornography, also heavy metal rock and roll concerts, the acceptance of deviant sexual life styles. They also show Racial inequality.

The representatives close the presentation with a warning that they feel that the threat of fire from heaven is very real and should not be scoffed at, and that they are pleading with them to go as quickly as possible to the safe zone in Israel, and release their animals from any service contracts, or bring their animals with them. The animals must be free to choose to flee as well.

The presentations are completed in four days and prepared for deployment. Azazel is trying to mitigate the coming presentations by speaking to as many people as possible, and giving them a completely different version of the event in Petra, of course they are lies. He claims that Jesus captured the representatives and has forced them to make a presentation and to lie in it, or they will lose their families. Azazel (Lucifer) implies that the horrible clips are actually from Jesus's home planet, not the earth.

The presentations are to be deployed in the sky starting at the edge of the frontier and moving in towards Jerusalem from there. There are fifty systems for projecting the images, the program will last for one half hour and then move inward to a predetermined location and show again. This process will repeat itself over again until everyone in the kingdom has had an opportunity to see it.

The initial results are abysmal, the people are so hardened in their views that they generally turned and walked away before the presentation was even complete. The animals were much more responsive than the people, they don't receive what Azazel has been saying, they have started the long journey back to Jerusalem. The loss of the animals and their labor has enraged the Enoshe and they are angry with the Government, there have been mobs of men breaking into the offices of the saints and ELE in the settlements. The saints and Enoshe law enforcement officers are evacuating from the settlements as the presentation moves by, they assist the animals and people who want to flee.

CHAPTER FOURTEEN

The Final Battle

It's been two weeks since the presentations have started showing, they are now much closer to Israel and the camp of the saints. The border line of the camp has now been delineated all the way around, and consists of two fences, the outer fence is six feet high with no wire to make it dangerous to climb over, but the second fence is eight feet high and has a defensive barrier on top. The area between the two fences is labeled as a "no go zone" and is about one hundred yards wide. There are many gates in the fences, there are walkways between the fences to direct traffic to the gates of the second fence. There are guards stationed at the gates, they are saints and angels, nobody knows just how many are there, only a few are visible at any one time.

Azazel has been sending his agents to the camp in an attempt to infiltrate and terrorize the inhabitants. Jesus, has pulled all the ELE officers back into the Jerusalem area. This is to protect them from the rebellion, The Lord knows that the rebellion is against him and his kingdom, so the angels and saints are the first line of defense. everyone that is approaching the camp is observed and analyzed, as to whether or not they are a threat. If they are found to be a threat they are removed from the area, and sent back to their homes. When people came to the gates to flee the rebellion, they were required to confirm their fidelity to the Lord's kingdom.

The settlements which are closer to the safe zone had begun coming to the area very quickly, these people were very devout and had been warned through prayer, by the Holy Spirit to flee to safety, they did not require the presentation to get the message.

At times during the past thousand years, there has been tens of thousands of saints living and working in the Jerusalem area, after all, they were helping to run the Lord's government. But, recently the numbers of saints in and around Jerusalem has been reduced to a fraction of the normal numbers.

David Bet Audee-El the son of Gus has noticed this reduction and was beginning to be concerned. He has approached Thomas Taylor and asked, "Do you know what is going on?

Thomas, hesitates, then drops his head, as though in prayer, then looks up and smiles at David, "Yes, I can tell you, there is a most amazing event coming soon, the Lord is going to remove his kingdom from the surface of the earth, and relocate it to the third heavens in one continuous action."

David exclaims, "Why? I thought that the safe zone would be excluded from the fire, which will come to purge the earth."

Thomas replies, "Yes, the safe zone will be protected during the event until the kingdom is gone, then the walls will be dropped and the air will feed the fire. The first heavens, or atmosphere will be sucked into the fire and will feed the flames, the oceans will be evaporated and completely dried, the oceans will be gone." [60]

Thomas continues, "The heat from the world wide fire will begin melting the surface of the earth, the mountains and elements will melt."

David asks, "How will the earth support life and people live here?

Thomas sighs, then replies, "It won't, at least not for a while, we will return at a later time, but not right away.

David, do you remember how the church of Jesus Christ was changed, in the twinkling of an eye and caught up to heaven, to become the bride of Christ? The Enoshe within the safety zone will be changed just like the church was and then taken to the third heavens. The saints are being relocated to the third heaven first, to reduce the traffic on that day, and provide space for the rural Enoshe to enter Jerusalem. When that day is over, there will be no Enoshe left at all. Fallen mankind will be completely gone from the earth, the redeemed Enoshe have been moved to the third heavens, and all the works of fallen man, Enoshe are gone."

David asks, "What about the animals? What will happen to them?"

Thomas smiled and says, "I can't tell you much, but you need to understand that the Lord came back to earth from heaven on the back of a horse, in fact I was also riding a horse. These horses were able to move thru the sky and survive without air. There are animals in heaven, and they are indeed very special."

David asks, "When will it happen, when will the fire come?

Thomas says, "No one is sure, the decision is the Lords, and no one knows what will trigger it. We all know that he can be trusted to do it, or not, at the right time and for the right reason."

Azazel is monitoring the flow of people to the saint's camp, and accessing how strong his rebellion is. He has ordered his people to move to the camp as quickly as possible, and from every direction at the same time. He has given very specific orders not to attempt to enter the saint's camp, till they are told.

Azazel believes that if the density of the rebellion on all the boarders of the camp, is great enough, it will be impossible to stop the masses of people from overwhelming the fences and defenses of Gods strong hold. But he must hold back the rebels till the numbers are sufficient.

It is nearly noon day in Israel and the camp of the saints. There are no clouds in the sky, there is an eerie silence around the camp, you could cut the tension with a knife. The rebels are looking into the enclosure, past the guard locations and as far as they can see into the camp, but they see no one. There is only an occasional flock of birds flying at top speed into the camp, they just disappear into the distance, within the enclosure, it's like they were late for Noah's ark.

Azazel receives word that his people are in place all the way around the Jewish settlements, Israel, and the city of Jerusalem. The distance around is hundreds of miles in length, the rebels are like the sands of the sea, as far as one can see.

Azazel gives the order to attack, and not to stop no matter what happens, the time is noon exactly. All of Azazel's commanders have been told to give the same order at the same time.

The huge rebel cry is heard as they begin to press forward into God's camp, the first fence crumples easily and the masses move on to the second fence, as soon as they touch it there is a loud sound of thunder from overhead.

Because of the frenzy of the people up in the front attack, they can not stop or look around, they just keep pressing forward. But, the people further back in the throng can see very clearly that there is a wall, which looks like the shimmering wall of the northern lights coming down from the top of the atmosphere, flowing down like sheets of flames, white, like plasma.

Overhead of the camp of the saints a huge portal is opening up in the second heavens making way to travel directly into the third heavens. There is a mighty rush of wind going up into the opening, The wind storm takes about five minutes to evacuate the camp, and then the portal closed behind the wind, the closure of the portal caused a horrific clap of thunder. Then as the flames reached the ground around the camp, and all sounds inside stopped, everything went silent, without oxygen sound cannot travel. The cries of the rebels can not be heard as they simply crumple in place.

The fire from heaven continues to flow down, when it hits the surface it flows like water, outward from the camp, like a fifty-foot-high flaming tsunami of flammable fuel. The same process is happening from five other portals located around the world. The oceans very quickly begin to boil away. The ice caps don't last long under the extreme temperatures. There is no throttle on the rate of combustion, thus the atmosphere itself is beginning to burn off, the situation is so bad that the surface elements begin to melt, and the whole earth is incinerated.

Nothing is left alive; the earth is finished.

CHAPTER FIFTEEN

The Great White Throne [61]

The great rush of wind that was heard leaving the camp of the saints, and going up into the portal in the sky, was the spiritual removal of God's people.

David Bet Audee-El finds himself among a multitude of people, arrayed inside a very large room, they are in the position to observe the proceedings.

The room itself is the Judgement hall of God, it is also called the great white throne judgment. God the father, the Ancient of Days, is sitting at the center on a throne, and the Elect One, Jesus the Christ is on a throne to his right.

The observers are saints, and they are coming and going from the hall. There is no cheering, shouting of excitement by the observers, they understand the gravity of the situation. They've been told that the first defendant to be tried will be the angel Hey-lel, he and his angel rebellion, will be cast into the lake of fire.

Next, the two hundred Ben-Elohim watchers, which mated with Enoshe women, then the spirits of the Nephilim which existed before the flood, the demons, followed by the Rephiam giants of the post flood times. And, finally the spirits of the Enoshe, mankind, who had died without a relationship with Jesus, they did not apply the blood sacrifice of Jesus Christ, from the cross to their sin, these people, died in their sin. The last group of these people are the rebels which had just died in the fire from heaven.

All of the guilty angels, spirits and people are going to be cast into the lake that burns with fire.

The devout believers in Christ, who lived by faith and gave their lives to him, those who had accepted his atonement for their sins, are not judged at the Great White Throne, they are saved. And will be judged at the judgment seat of Christ, not for sin but for rewards, for their obedience and faithfulness, their sins have been washed away.

The angels which had joined with Hey-lel in his rebellion about eleven thousand years ago are lining up on the left side of the throne, and are waiting to go before God. The angels had failed to present themselves before God, back at the beginning, and had since been used by Hey-lel to attack and destroy mankind over a six-thousand-year time period, their crimes are numerous. These angels have just had their trials, in open chambers proceeding off to the left of God's throne.

A combination of saints and angels are conducting the trials, reviewing all the evidence and hearing testimony concerning the charges. Then a judgment is announced and the defendant is moved to the line for sentencing by the Ancient of Days on the throne. Many of the angels just waive their right to a full trial when they hear the charges and see the people that they violated when they were working with Hey-lel, they simply admit their guilt and walk on.

The judgment at the great white throne is going take a long time, there are billions to be tried. Time in heaven is different than on earth, it is not sequenced by the sun, there are no days as it is on earth. All those (angel, spirit or person) found guilty at the judgment will be led off to the lake that burns with fire

There are no people or animals on earth, all the spirits have come to heaven for judgement and relocation to their eternal abodes. The earths surface is burned and melted, the mountains have fallen down, and there are no more oceans, lakes or seas. The sky is gone, the first heaven is passed away. There is no air to breathe and no blue sky.

It is going to be a long time before the earth recovers. David walks out of the judgment hall and sees some trees in a field of grass off to his right. He thinks to himself, *"I don't recognize those trees, I wonder what they are?"*

As he turns to walk that way, he suddenly realizes that he is there, standing next to the tree, whoa! He exclaims. "How did that happen?"

Just as he says that, He hears a voice behind him, it is Thomas Taylor,

Thomas say's "I'm sorry David, I am assigned to give you the first day orientation, and I didn't see you leave the hall. I see you have found how easy it is to travel here in heaven." Then Thomas laughed, and said, "Come with me I have something you need to see.

Thomas turns and beckons to David to follow him, and just like David's trip over to the tree, he and Thomas are instantly standing on a high hill overlooking a large valley.

David exclaims, "What is that? Its massive!"

Thomas replies, "I knew you would like it, this is the new Jerusalem, It's nearly complete. And now that the family of God is complete, and we are all here in heaven, no one missing, we can now complete the whole thing, a home for all of us." [62]

Thomas continues, "David, when we were in Petra, you will never know how hard it was for me, to not tell you what was going on here in heaven, and how close you were to going home. All of the dreams you had about the new heaven and the new earth, and new Jerusalem are happening right in front of you, the gates, the foundations, the river and the trees, it's all here."

David goes quiet, and is just staring across the valley. Thomas say's "I'll come back in a few moments."

Then David hears someone say, "David... David?"

David knows who it is! He swirls around and looks, yes, it's his father. Gus steps forward and looks David in the eye and tells him, "Well done son".

David's eyes instantly go to tears, and he says, "I'm changed Dad, Dad I'm changed, It's all really true! I'm changed just the way you taught me when I was little. it happened just like you said it would."

Gus says, "So, you're changed? Tell me about it." [63]

David says, "Well I can see perfectly, like an eagle, everything is super clear, and the colors here in heaven are beyond vivid. I can hear everything, the smallest sounds are clear as a bell, I can smell things that are all new and my nose is crazy sensitive."

He continues, "And while I am young again, I was never as strong as this, or anywhere near this agile, also my mind is in high gear, everything seems so simple and clear, this is all amazing, and Jesus did this, for me... for me."

The two men hugged and wept on each other's shoulders.

Then after a few moments Gus asked David, "Do you remember asking me, when you were young, about the seas being dried up on the earth, and you wanted to know, what about the whales and dolphins and fish? Well I know now, what the Lord is going to do, he's going to..."

JESUS CHRIST
WORLD WITHOUT END

REFERENCE LIST

[1] Scripture refer. Genesis 12:16 Jacobs ladder from heaven.

[2] Scripture refer. Joel 2:1-11 Joel's army, the army of God...

[3] Scripture refer. Joel 2:3 Garden in front and fire behind.

[4] Scripture refer. Isaiah 63:1 Who is this that cometh from Edom.

[5] Scripture refer. Ezekiel 1:4 Open clouds from heaven.

[6] Scripture refer. Revelation 19:11-13 The Lord comes on a horse.

[7] Scripture refer. Revelation 19:14 The bride comes on a horse also.

[8] Scripture refer. Isaiah 63:1 The Lord goes to Jerusalem.

[9] Scripture refer. Revelation 12:14 The seed of the woman to the place prepared.

[10] Scripture refer. Matthew 24:16 Those in Judaea flee to the mountains.

[11] Scripture refer. Revelation 13:17 No man might buy or sell.

[12] Scripture refer. Luke 21:20 Flee when you see Jerusalem surrounded.

[13] Scripture refer. Colossians 1:17 By him all things consist.

[14] Scripture refer. I Corinthians 15:42-44 Sow a natural body, raised a spiritual.

[15] Scripture refer. Ezekiel 1:16-19 A wheel within a wheel.

[16] Scripture refer. Micah 5:5-6 Messiah destroys Assyria, 15 chosen men.

[17] Scripture refer. Ezekiel 9:2,3,11 The angels with ink horn.

[18] Scripture refer. Matthew 12:36-37 By every word.

[19] Scripture refer. Ezekiel 1:26 A platform for God's throne.

[20] Scripture refer. Hebrews 1:8 The Lord's Scepter.

[21] Scripture refer. Jude 1:6 & II Peter 2:4 Angels in chains.

[22] Scripture refer. Genesis 6:2 Angels marry human daughters.

[23] Scripture refer. Enoch 15:8-10 Evil spirits from giants.

[24] Scripture refer. Jubilees 10:11 Lord binds 90% of the demons, leaves 10%.

[25] Scripture refer. Micah 5:5-6 Assyria destroyed when Lord returns.

[26] Scripture refer. Isaiah 62:2 & Revelations 2:17 A new name written.

[27] Scripture refer. Revelation 7:3-8 The Tribes are sealed.

[28] Scripture refer. Matthew 6:10 Thy kingdom come thy will be done in earth.

[29] Scripture refer. I kings 8:10-11 The Lords glory comes down.

[30] Scripture refer. Jubilees 6:32-35 The 364-day calendar ordained.

[31] Scripture refer. Jubilees 3:28 The animals could talk.

[32] Scripture refer. Revelation 20:1-3 Satan is bound for 1000 years.

[33] Scripture refer. Jubilees 23:27-29 Aging process slow down.

[34] Scripture refer. Enoch 72:8-22 Enoch's 364-day calendar.

[35] Scripture refer. Jubilees 3:28 The animals can talk.

[36] Scripture refer. Jubilees 6:36-37 The Lunar calendar is wrong.

[37] Scripture refer. Ezekiel 47:1-9 The dead sea is healed.

[38] Scripture refer. Ezekiel 47:10 The shore line up to En-gedi.

[39] Scripture refer. Ezekiel 47:1 The river flows from the temple.

[40] Scripture refer. Ezekiel 42:16-20 The temple site 500 reeds square.

[41] Scripture refer. Hebrews 1:8 The Lord's scepter.

[42] Scripture refer. Revelation 2:17 The Hidden manna.

[43] Scripture refer. Jubilees 2:17-20 The Lord's Shabbat day.

[44] Scripture refer. Zechariah 14:16-19 The feast of tabernacles.

[45] Scripture refer. Jubilees 19:8 Abrahams ten trials.

[46] Scripture refer. Revelations 4:1 Future visions.

[47] Scripture refer. Jubilees 4:33 Noah's wife Emzara.

[48] Scripture refer. Jubilees 12:25-27 Abram learns Hebrew.

[49] Scripture refer. Jubilees 11:15-16 Abram forsakes the Idols.

[50] Scripture refer. Jubilees 17:17 Abraham's ten trials.

[51] Scripture refer. I John 3:2 We will be like him.

[52] Scripture refer. Jubilees 12:12-14 Fire burns demon temple in Ur.

[53] Scripture refer. Jubilees 10:11 10% of the demons remain for Satan.

[54] Scripture refer. Jubilees 12:12-14 Haran, Abraham's brother is killed.

[55] Scripture refer. Ezekiel 28:15 Satan's iniquity found.

[56] Scripture refer. Revelation 20:2-3 Satan is loosed from incarceration.

[57] Scripture refer. Genesis 5:27 Methuselah lives 969 years.

[58] Scripture refer. Zechariah 14:17-19 Droughts and plagues.

[59] Scripture refer. Revelation 20:7-8 Satan deceives the people.

[60] Scripture refer. Revelation 21:1 There is no more sea.

[61] Scripture refer Revelation 20:11 The great white throne.

[62] Scripture refer. Revelation 21:2 The new Jerusalem.

[63] Scripture refer. I John 3:2 & I Corinthians 15:42-44 God will change us.

[64] Scripture refer. I Chronicles 17:11 The Davidic covenant from God, the everlasting kingdom.

Printed in the United States
By Bookmasters